The Primate Puzzle

A tale of two friends and the
missing long-nosed monkeys

by
Oliver Renier Nash

**Illustrations and Cover
by
Bethanie Cunnick**

authorHOUSE®

AuthorHouse™ UK Ltd.
500 Avebury Boulevard
Central Milton Keynes, MK9 2BE
www.authorhouse.co.uk
Phone: 08001974150

First published by AuthorHouse 7/1/2010

ISBN: 978-1-4490-3983-7 (e)
ISBN: 978-1-4490-3099-5 (sc)

This book is printed on acid-free paper.

For all of my family and friends
Far and wide
Past and Present

iii

Without Great Ormond Street Hospital for Children I would not be here. All author and illustrator profits are being donated to the best children's hospital in the world. Thank you for all you have done and all the wonderful work you continue to do.

Oliver Renier Nash

CHAPTER ONE

This tale begins on a dark and gloomy Saturday. The rain was swooping down in sheets and the wind was howling outside the windows. On this dismal morning, Amy Applegate was sitting at the dining room table waiting for her breakfast. Just so you do not think this tale is about a spoilt little girl in a posh mansion, waiting for her butler, let me quickly explain. Every Saturday in the Applegate household on Cuckoo Lane, Amy's father Tom started work later than usual. He always cooked them a hearty breakfast as a treat.

On this particular Saturday, Amy had polished off a bowl of her favourite cereal 'Choco-Snaps'. Only a small bowl though, as she knew how large these breakfasts always were. This morning was no exception: a sausage, crispy bacon, tomatoes, fresh mushrooms and eggy bread, which Tom called French toast but Amy knew it was made in the kitchen not France.

After breakfast, Amy stared out of the window at the dark clouds launching lightning down to earth. Tom had gone to the kitchen to clear up and had not detected the bored face gazing out of the window. Amy did not like the rain and murky weather. She was not a *Playstation* girl, she preferred the outdoors. If it were sunny, she would run round the corner and call on her best friend George.

Still daydreaming, she had not noticed her mother Kelly returning from her jog. Kelly walked into the room drenched and saw the faraway look on her daughter's face. After a soggy hug, her mother asked, 'Why don't you do some painting or read one of your books, sweetheart?' She did as her mother suggested and found her painting materials, spreading her things out on the lounge floor. Normally Amy's sister, Bethany, would be treading all over her stuff and pestering her. It was not that Bethany was a horrid little sister but she was a tinkerer. Whatever Amy touched, Bethany touched. Whatever Amy was doing, Bethany wanted to be part of it. At Christmas, Bethany would enjoy playing with Amy's presents much more than her own. Bethany doted over her big sister but they could fight like cat and dog. Amy loved her sister but did enjoy the peace and quiet when Bethany stayed over at Grandma Jenny's house.

Amy's painting soon took shape. It was of a vast, dazzling, honey coloured sun surrounded by dancing clouds and birds carrying worms to their chicks. She had a real talent for art especially when drawing or painting animals. Amy began imagining herself out amongst the trees, listening to the birds singing and chasing around the fields with George. Tom interrupted her daydreaming with a kiss on the cheek before heading out the door. He was about to close the door when he turned to Amy and said, 'As you like animals so much, why don't you try the puzzle on the back of the cereal box? It's not going to stop raining and you might win something.' Amy was intrigued and it was truly miserable outside. She left her paints strewn across the floor and went to take a peek at the cereal box.

CHOCO-SNAPS CEREALS and FLYAWAY AIRLINES are giving *you* the chance to win the holiday of a lifetime. Win a trip for two to see these animals whilst visiting some of the most remarkable places on earth:

**Observe the monitor lizards in
AUSTRALIA
Swim with turtles in INDONESIA
Watch pink flamingos in SINGAPORE
See the giant Asian Elephants in
THAILAND**

However, these were not the captions or picture that caught Amy's eye!

Help care for injured and orphaned orangutans in
BORNEO

Amy had never seen such an adorable or attractive young animal as this in her entire life. She fell in love with this beguiling young orangutan, although she had no idea where Borneo was. All that stood in her way was one, small, tiny, little puzzle! This was not going to stop her from feeding a baby orangutan. Instantly she was rushing around, almost knocking over her mother in her frantic search to find a pen that would win her the ultimate prize. Her competitive streak shone brightly, this was one prize she must try to win!

With her pen in hand, Amy began circling all the animal names that she could find. She soon forgot about her painting. They went up, down, side to side and even diagonally. Choco-Snaps had given each contestant a one animal head-start – ELEPHANT. Her parents had taken her and George to Colchester and London Zoo many times. Amy chuckled to herself as she remembered how George had been great at imitating the animal noises, although it caused a squabble or two. There were some Japanese tourists reading the information panel by the tiger enclosure. George was only ten metres away mimicking an elephant call to confuse them. The tourists started to argue with each other over who should be reading the English signs, as it was clearly an elephant they should be looking for and not a tiger. The more animals Amy found, the more of George's impressions she remembered from those outings. She was certain of one thing. She would invite George to go with her *if* she got lucky and won, as she could never choose between her parents as to who would accompany her. That was one choice she definitely did not want to make. The time flew by and Amy found so many different animals; monkey, snake, lizard, frog, bat, cat, rat, leopard and crocodile to name but a few. She even found an upside down chimpanzee. Eventually, she looked up at the clock and to her surprise it was almost time for her father to get back from work. She had been so engrossed that she had forgotten the rain and most of the day had flown by.

D	R	I	B	B	G	O	R	F	D
R	C	O	W	A	M	Y	L	O	R
A	T	A	R	A	T	D	G	X	I
Z	O	C	A	T	E	N	O	O	B
L	D	O	G	N	G	A	A	L	E
L	E	O	P	A	R	D	T	A	L
C	A	R	A	H	O	R	A	F	I
N	M	E	D	P	E	A	E	F	D
E	A	G	N	E	G	E	L	U	O
X	L	I	A	L	B	B	F	B	C
O	L	T	P	E	K	A	N	S	O
M	O	N	K	E	Y	A	P	E	R
E	E	Z	N	A	P	M	I	H	C

Soon afterwards Tom walked through the front door and upon seeing the completed puzzle he exclaimed, 'Wow, you found loads. I honestly think you've found every last one of them. You are a clever little monkey, aren't you?'

Amy was so excited about entering the competition until she noticed some tiny writing at the bottom of the entry form. Amy let out a shriek before reading it to her parents, 'All competitors must be twelve years of age or over! What am I going to do?' She dropped the Choco-snaps in bitter disappointment, spilling cereal all over the table.

Her mother wanted to tell her off but instead picked up the box for a closer look. Kelly read the box, 'I think you might be okay. You're eleven years, 10 months and 20 odd days old,' the type of guesstimate only a mother would get so close. 'The closing date for the competition is in eight weeks time. As long as we don't post it until maybe a week before your birthday, your entry will be valid. Now, can you clean up this table my girl?'

Amy was immediately reassured, 'Please, please, please don't forget to post it. I worked so hard on that word search.' Kelly made a point of marking the date to post her entry in bright red pen on the David Beckham calendar as a final reminder.

During the next week, Amy ate an awful lot of Choco-Snaps so that the box could be cut up and the puzzle put in an envelope ready to post. On the entry form Amy marked the boxes, Australia NO, Singapore NO, Indonesia No, Thailand NO and Borneo, YES! Her heart was set on helping the orangutans.

Over the next few months Amy was busy at school and preoccupied with her upcoming birthday. At school she pestered her teachers with questions about Borneo, rainforests, animals, swamps, plants, trees and creepy-crawly insects. Her parents were worried about Amy getting her hopes up too high about winning. They knew that tens of thousands of children around the country would have entered this competition. Choco-Snaps were the most popular cereal in the country and a box was sitting in most kitchen cupboards. To soften the anticipated blow, they bought her an animal encyclopaedia. Amy learnt so many new facts from her lessons at school and her book. Everyday she would bombard her family with astonishing facts.

Monday – 'Mum, did you know that in Venezuela the tribesmen often settle disputes with chest–pounding duels.'

Tuesday – 'Dad, the Amazon River is over 4,000 miles long.'

Wednesday – 'Uncle Olly, have you heard about the frogs that can fly?'

He replied with a smile, 'Yes, I'd heard that some frogs have webbed feet and hands which act as a parachute when they glide, not fly, between trees. This allows them to escape from predators!'

'Oh, Uncle Olly, you're such a know it all!'

Thursday – 'Grandma Jenny, an adult elephant drinks 225 litres of water every day.'

'Aren't you becoming a little naturalist?' replied Grandma Jenny. Amy was curious as to what exactly a naturalist was. Her grandparents had always insisted, 'If you need to ask, ask. If that person doesn't know, ask someone else or get a library book to help you. There is no harm in being inquisitive.' Grandma Jenny explained that a naturalist was someone who studies all different types of plants and animals.

Her Grandfather Peter joined in the conversation, 'Amy, did YOU know that an elephant goes for a wee every twenty minutes because it drinks so much water?'

'Now you're just being silly aren't you?' answered Amy, as he winked at her.

It was Amy's turn to annoy her little sister by bombarding her with constant facts. Bethany loved animals too but she did not understand a lot of the stuff Amy was telling her, so she got bored pretty quickly. Unlike George, Amy was one of those children that actually appeared to enjoy school. Where else could you spend all day with your friends, talk, read books, learn, paint and get time to play different sports?

Weeks had gone by, her twelfth birthday had come and gone and everyone had forgotten about the competition. One evening, after Amy had been visiting a school friend, she arrived back for supper to find a letter next to her tablemat. The letter had arrived in the post after Amy had left for school. Her parents were dying for her to get home and open it. She tore open the letter and began to read:

CHOCO-SNAPS CEREALS
&
FLYAWAY AIRLINES

Would like to congratulate: - **AMY APPLEGATE** on winning our recent word search competition. You have won a holiday for two to Malaysian Borneo. We will fly you First Class to Borneo. In Borneo a guide will meet you at the airport and accompany you for the entire magical holiday. During your stay you will visit an orangutan rehabilitation centre, where you will help care for injured and orphaned orangutans.

You will trek into the rainforest and go on boat trips in search of fantastic wildlife and rare plants. An Orang Ulu tribesman will teach you many of their ancient traditions. You will stay in a traditional longhouse - an entire village under one roof. Spend a night camping in a famous cave and much, much more.

Please contact our company representative in the next few days to discuss the arrangements. BLAH, BLAH, BLAH was all Amy read after that because she was overcome by happiness. She jumped up and down with the letter in her hand. 'I've won, I've won, I've really won,' she roared at the top of her voice. Bethany got scared by Amy's weird behaviour and deafening shouts so stormed off to her room in a huff.

Although it was not the first thing Amy had won, it certainly was the most exciting. Does a pink rosette for first place in a local beautiful baby contest even count? Her parents were delighted for her but had many questions that needed to be answered. Amy was not thinking about problems, she wanted to tell George she had just won something big, no make that huge. Tom and Kelly put aside their initial concerns so as not to spoil the happiest moment of their young daughter's life. They sat at the table laughing, as their daughter danced, bounded, leapt, hopped and frolicked around like a mad Morris dancer. Amy waltzed around the lounge in a whirlwind of delight.

CHAPTER TWO

The next day at school Amy was the centre of attention and the day passed in the blink of an eye. Many of her school friends could not believe how jammy she was in winning the competition. However, we know that luck only had a small part to play. Amy thought it was down to 50% perseverance, 45% due to the awful English weather and maybe just 5% luck. By the time the school bell rang to mark the end of the day, you can be certain Amy was very tired of answering one question in particular. School children being school children the same the whole world over, *everyone* must have asked her at least once, some twice or even more, 'Amy, can I please, please come with you on this holiday? Honestly, I'll be your best friend forever!'

They could ask until they were blue in the face but Amy was certain and had already made her mind up. If his parents would let him, then she wanted George to go with her. Fingers crossed, he would come and they would have a great adventure with laughter being high on the menu each day.

That evening Tom arranged for George and his parents, Helen and Andy, to come over for dinner to discuss the options and formulate a plan. Amy's grandparents, who lived round the corner, were looking after Bethany and George's younger brother Vincent. Both sets of parents were concerned about many aspects of the trip, not least the fact that they were both very young to be flying on their own. The nerve-racking reality of letting their children jet off, thousands of miles, to feed orangutans was beginning to set in.

'Well done Amy! I'm so proud of you for winning the competition,' said Helen on arrival.

George bolted through the door right behind her, all smiles, bouncing around like *Tigger*. 'It's blooming marvellous, brilliant, unbelievable. In fact, it's the cat's meow!'

'I haven't heard you use that one before George?' said Amy.

'It's new. I kept getting in trouble for saying everything was the mutt's n…'

'George! Hold your horses young man, we've a lot to discuss before we let you go gallivanting half way around the world,' said Andy.

'But, but we're old enough ….' stammered Amy and George in unison before Kelly stopped the conversation by calling everyone for dinner.

After dinner Tom telephoned the company representative about the prize, he switched it on to speakerphone so they could all hear the replies. As Amy and George were unaccompanied minors, the company had made arrangements for an airline rep to look after them from check-in at London until boarding. After that, they would be flying first class and be looked after by the flight attendants. The airline would ensure they were escorted through immigration and stay with them until they were handed over to the guide. They did not need any vaccine injections, but had to visit the doctor and take a few sugars cubes with medicine on to protect them from rabies. Both mothers winced at the mere mention of rabies but the children smiled at missing out on any jabs. They were told their guide's name was Izwan Izwani and she would be with them for the duration of the holiday. Questions were asked as to what should be packed; the list included waterproof jackets, torches and binoculars. However, they would be supplied with any camping gear and leech socks by their guide!

'Leech socks!' the two mothers blurted out in harmony.

'Why on earth would they need leech socks?' said Helen.

'There are leeches in the rainforest but they are harmless, or so I'm told,' said the representative in a reassuring tone.

Amy could see the worried look on their faces so quickly added, 'Please don't worry. In the book you gave me it says they aren't dangerous and were once used by doctors to cure illnesses. As long as we keep our shirts tucked in and leech socks on, then it won't be a problem.'

George took his chance, he wanted to move the subject swiftly along from leech socks and on to a parent friendly question, 'Hello sir, George Cooke now speaking. We don't want to miss any school, so can we go at the beginning of our summer holiday, please?'

'All you need is a letter signed by your parents, with the most suitable dates for you to fly on. Then you'll be ready to enjoy the adventure of a lifetime. Can I help you with anything else?'

The four parents looked from one to another quizzically.

Amy replied for all of them, 'We have all the info we need to know at the moment, so thanks for your help. You've been ace!'

The young man at the end of the line wished them both a happy and safe trip. Before hanging up he teased them, saying he would gladly go in their place if they were not allowed to go.

Amy turned to their parents and asked, 'Is it okay if we go, *please*? We promise to behave and look after each other.'

Well, what could any parent say to such an appeal? Their immediate fears had been put to rest, except the thought of blood sucking leeches lurking in the undergrowth. Of course their parents agreed! Amy and George were in seventh heaven and could not wait to be adventurers, explorers and world travellers.

In the months leading up to the end of the school year both their homes became a hive of activity, making sure the children had everything ready. Both had been reading up on the exotic animals they might encounter and the country's peculiar plants. Their parents thought it might be nice if they learnt a few Malay words – hello, goodbye, yes, no, thank you, where is the toilet … etc. A few words can make a big difference when in a foreign land. It would be a good lesson for them and a good habit to get into.

Finally the school year finished and Amy sprinted home as fast as her legs would carry her. George was also delighted to see the back of the school year. He thought secondary school would be a breeze as he was sporty and one of the brightest students at his primary school; however this counted for nothing at his new school. In the first week some boys in the year above had decided to pick on him and put him upside down in a large playground bin filled with all-sorts of stinky rubbish. It did not stop there, for some reason this particular group of lads seemed to take every opportunity to bully George. George could not understand why they would do this, perhaps he had looked at them wrongly when he was having a kick around in the playground or perhaps they were just bored.

George's new friends always seemed to disappear into the shadows when the lads from the years above appeared. The bullies told him not to grass them or things would only get worse. George worked hard to avoid the bullies but he never felt settled at his new school because of these idiots. When they found out he was going on this exotic holiday it got worse; their jealousy made them pick on George even more than usual.

George wished he was stronger because being bullied by these morons stank, big-time! He hated lying to his Mum about why he had a ripped shirt or why he had lost text books that needed replacing. This holiday to Borneo had kept him going for the final few months of term and he could not wait to get on that aeroplane and forget all about school.

George and Amy had packed, repacked, checked and double-checked their rucksacks. They were both finally ready to go. Tom and Andy drove George and

Vincent to the airport and Amy went with her mother, Helen and Bethany.

Andy turned to George when they were nearing the airport and said, 'Tom and I have bought you and Amy a small going away present *but* it comes with some rules. Firstly, you and Amy must stick together and look after each other at *all* times. Secondly, you must not treat this as a toy because it can be dangerous!' This was enough to get George hooked and he almost interrupted. 'Thirdly, don't tell your Mum or Amy's Mum until you get back because they are already worried about you two leaving.'

George was thrilled with these conditions and it made him feel very grown up, 'No problem at all! Amy is my best friend on the planet, so we'll stick together like glue. And even I can keep a secret for an hour but I don't know what it is yet?'

Vincent was looking out the car window ignoring them all because he was not getting a present or as much attention as usual. George opened the pouch his father passed him and found the most gadget filled penknife he had ever seen: - a compass, a mini-saw, scissors, a small blade, a big blade and some things he had no idea what they were for.

'This is the best, most splendiferous present ever. Thanks heaps, Tom! Cheers Dad,' said George before delivering a high-five, which made a crisp slap on contact.

'We both agreed that if you were going on a boy scouts trip you might need one, but if you're going on an expedition into a rainforest you would definitely need one. We don't like to keep secrets from our wives but it's for the best. So pack both of them away in your check-in rucksack and not your hand luggage! Oh and don't forget to tell Amy the rules when you arrive,' Tom added.

'Also George, don't try and bring back anything dodgy! Remember what happened at Gatwick airport after last summer's holiday. The customs officer gave you a right ear full for hiding those contraband bangers in with the chocolate slices. Your Mum was also less than impressed,' said Andy, in an exasperated tone of voice. George managed not to smile by thinking about what a terrible waste it was. All those euros he had spent on high-quality, finger length bangers only to get them confiscated at the last minute.

In the other car, Amy was in high spirits and was getting her last minute pointers from the two Mums. Bethany was miserable because she wanted to go with her big sister; she had already cried herself dry that morning.

Helen began, 'We know we don't need to remind you about these rules but George is being told the same things, right now.' She was very mistaken because George was admiring his penknife and listening to The Beatles blaring out of the car stereo. 'Always treat people, as you would like them to treat you. People like children who listen, smile and are polite.' Amy half-heartedly promised to be on her best behaviour. She was getting butterflies; this was going to be more difficult leaving her family than she first thought.

As they arrived at the airport, Kelly added, 'Sweetheart, always remember that good manners cost nothing.'

We will not dwell on what happened inside the airport because saying goodbye to people you love is always melancholy. A kind lady called Doris checked in their baggage and found a flight attendant, called Shirley, to show them onboard the Flyaway Airlines Aeroplane. First Class was incredible because one minute they were sad saying good-bye to their parents and the next they were occupied by a massive selection of computer games and movies. Shirley made sure they were well fed and always had a drink. A few people in First Class looked at Amy and George with some astonishment. I suppose it would be a strange sight to see two twelve year olds having the time of their lives, travelling on their *own* in expensive luxury seats.

After a few hours of playing on the in-flight entertainment and watching movies they both dozed off. They slept soundly due to all the excitement they had had that day. They awoke to find themselves about to land in Kota Kinabalu in Borneo, having not even noticed that most of the passengers had disembarked at Kuala Lumpur.

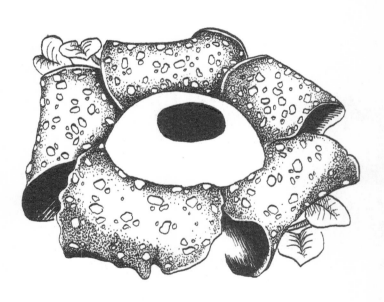

CHAPTER THREE

On arrival, Shirley the flight attendant escorted them through passport control and along to the baggage collection area to wait for their bags. She nipped away to speak to a customs officer she knew, who promised her he would rush them through without any hassle. When she returned she pointed out the customs man in the distance and the door leading to the arrivals area. She told George and Amy that their guide would be waiting there with a sign with their names on. She was obviously in a rush and asked if they minded her leaving them. She was shortly due to catch another aeroplane to Bangkok, Thailand. When they nodded their agreement, she thanked them before darting off with her mini-suitcase wheeling behind her. They did not even get the chance to thank her properly.

They were alone for the first time this holiday, smiling but nervously excited as to what might lay ahead. They had not been standing there long and were paying no attention to the bags rotating round and round the baggage carousel, when a hulking bear of a man shoved them aside to grab his immense bag. He knocked Amy off her feet when he clumsily pushed back past them to load the bag onto his trolley.

If that was not bad enough, a spiteful looking woman with a hook nose, fierce grey eyes and a baseball cap barged passed to grab the next bag from the busy carousel.

'Excuse me, there's no need to push!' objected George, angry at their behaviour, knocking Amy over and not batting an eyelid. People think children behave badly but sometimes adults are even worse!

'*Excuse you*! You snotty first class brats! You should look where you're bleedin' going!' scowled the woman. She then turned on Amy, 'Poor diddums, no-one around to carry your bags? No-one around to pick the little lady up off 'er backside? Where have your servants disappeared off to? I know; they're hiding. Probably need a break from you two whining brats. I'd lend you my useless hunk of lard but I don't think he likes children unless they're on toast'.

The gargantuan, unshaven man took the bag off her and tossed it effortlessly onto the trolley. He slowly turned around to George and whispered in a menacing tone, 'You two posh kids should be very careful. It's a jungle out there and dangerous if you're on your own! So remember, don't get lost.' He let out an ominous laugh and made two of his fingers into a gun shape before pointing them at George. He fired, making a childish exploding noise before winking and abruptly storming off behind the woman.

George offered Amy his hand to pull her up off the floor. They stared at each other in utter disbelief. 'Did you smell those two chumps? They stank of booze and had the manners of a crocodile!' huffed George, feeling pretty ruffled.

'I didn't like that one bit. What about telling the customs man or the guide that he threatened you?'

'Don't worry about it Amy, we'll grab our bags and be having loads of fun in no time. Forget them; they're just a couple of drunken fools in a hurry! The Hulk and Hooknose, what a pair of stinkers!'

They breezed through customs, giving the customs man a wave before heading to the arrivals area. An ample woman greeted them with a beaming smile holding a sign with their names on it, as promised.

'Hi! You must be Amy and this handsome young man must be George' - he instantly began to blush. 'My name is Izwan Izwani but you can call me Izzy. I'm going to be your guide for the holiday. I'm sure we're going to have lots of fun together!'

'Selamat Pagi,' they both replied, 'good morning'.

Izzy let out a giggle of delight before answering them back in Malay. She then scooped up their bags, 'Come on then, let's chat on the way. My jeep is outside.'

On the way to their lodgings she began to explain what activities were planned. Today would be fairly relaxed because they had been on the aeroplane for so long. Izzy was unsure what effect the time difference would have on them. When it is midday in England it is 8pm in Borneo; this time change can cause people to feel unwell or disorientated for a few days. Izzy explained this problem and said it was called 'jet lag'. Therefore on arrival at the lodge, which was situated next to a river and an enormous rainforest, she suggested that they unpack and relax until lunchtime. After lunch she would take them for their first trek into the rainforest to show them a few of the local plants and animals.

Whilst unpacking the essentials George turned to Amy and said, 'I can see you've got most things out ready for this afternoon's trek but here is something our dads bought for us. We each got a little going away present.' This was a pleasant surprise. She was a little shocked upon opening it, as she was not expecting a penknife with tons of gadgets. George quickly told her of the conditions attached to the present, 'No mucking around with it because it's dangerous, we must look after each other, blah, blah, blah. You get the idea, the usual sort of stuff!'

'These are bound to come in handy!' replied Amy.

'So Amy, do you accept these conditions, *Deal or No Deal?*'

'Well Noel, I've had a great time and it's a fair offer so it's a deal!'

Before they set off in to the rainforest, Izzy made them put on their leech socks. They had a good laugh because these huge white cloth socks looked like old ladies' stockings, coming up to the children's knees. However, as Izzy was keen to point out, it was better to look daft once in the forest rather than having to burn off a bloodsucking leech from their legs or feet. It did not take her long to point out a massive Atlas moth hanging from a branch. Its wingspan was nearly thirty centimetres in diameter. The two children were dumbstruck at the variety of noises they heard. This was not like being in the park at home where they could hear the birds twittering, a dog barking or the wind rustling the leaves of a tree.

'Listen to the 'rainforest song' children. How many different sounds do you think you can hear,' enquired Izzy.

'Six,' guessed George, conservatively.

'Twelve to fourteen,' predicted Amy.

'Hundreds,' answered Izzy. 'In a rainforest you can hear hundreds of different birdcalls, crickets, grasshoppers, lizards, monkeys and many more.' She leaned across to one of the trees and picked off a bug not much bigger than a thimble. 'This is the cicada and it makes its call for many reasons. It's only the male who sings and he does this to attract a female mate, mark his territory or if he's being attacked. These noisy males all make slightly different sounds and there are literally millions of them in a rainforest.'

Izzy was pleased with the interest they showed and laughed when they both pointed out a plant saying it looked like it was from outer space. 'This is a meat-eating plant! It enjoys a breakfast of insects but can also feed on very small animals that get stuck inside. The bright colours and the sweet smell attract the pitcher plant's prey. Once the victims land on the surface they quickly slide down to their doom. Then they are digested in what would be the equivalent of the plant's stomach.'

Amy was quick to point out that the pitcher plant was similar to the Venus Flytrap. She had seen this in her book; the flytrap sprung its trap shut if an insect touched two of its feelers at the same time. George was less than impressed and thought it sounded gross.

Izzy was almost satisfied with the afternoon's work but really wanted to find one of the world's most famous plants to show them. She could see they were already covered with sweat. She knew it would take time for them to get used to the humidity in the rainforest, as well as the higher temperatures in Borneo. Izzy was about to turn back when amongst the thick undergrowth she spied the largest flower in the world. She pointed it out to Amy and George, who were stunned by its enormity. It was nearly one metre in diameter and had a blood red tinge to it. 'Have a sniff of the inner section,' said Izzy. 'It is absolutely delightful.'

Amy suggested that George go first because she thought it looked like a freaky flower from the *Day of the Triffids* that might come alive at any moment.

George edged closer, taking care not to tread on any of the surrounding flowers. He instantly got more than he bargained for, 'Blimey, what a stench! I haven't smelt anything that bad since we cleaned out my uncle's chicken shed!' He stepped back and made way for Amy.

She only gave it a delicate little sniff, 'Pooee, what a pong. That smells like rotten meat!'

Izzy was trying hard not to laugh but could not contain herself. She burst into laughter, scaring a few birds from their hiding places. In between fits of giggles she explained that the Rafflesia flower recreated the smell of exactly that, rotten meat. The worse it smelt the more flies and insects it attracted, meaning the bigger its lunch. The flower had mastered the skill so well that it grew to this world record size.

They began the trek back to the lodge and were almost at the clearing when Amy saw something high up in a tree, 'What is that?' said Amy, pointing it out to Izzy and George.

'It's got massive eyes,' added George.

'Well spotted, these particular animals are rarely seen or heard. It's called a slow loris but it isn't the slowest animal in the world. I think that award would go to one of the sloth family or maybe a koala bear. A loris is a species of lemur; this primate spends most of the day sleeping with its head between its legs and only becomes active around sunset. It will soon be searching for fruit, birds' eggs or fresh shoots.' He was not the most active or exciting animal they would encounter on their trip but it was a good start. The talk of food reminded the children how hungry they were. This was not an uncommon occurrence for George, as he was a typical growing lad who had the appetite of a horse. His father often joked that he must have tapeworms judging by the amount he ate.

They enjoyed a pleasant dinner together and agreed that an early night was in order. They had to leave at the crack of dawn the next morning to be at the orangutan rehabilitation centre for the first feeding. The children were happy about this as they were both tired and wanted to have a chat and fill in their journals before bed.

Once they had finished this and had a quick wash with the stored rainwater, they were ready for bed. They burrowed under their blankets and mosquito nets, wished each other goodnight and were asleep within seconds of their heads hitting the pillows.

CHAPTER FOUR

Izzy came and woke them quietly, telling them to creep towards the open shutters and look out. They certainly got a pleasant surprise; a fine-looking pair of rhinoceros hornbills were relaxing on a low branch at the edge of the clearing.

'This makes a lovely change for me,' George whispered, 'normally the only animal I see in the morning is next door's cat doing its business in my Mum's flower bed!'

Amy let out a muffled snigger at George, for his early morning crudeness.

After showering and breakfast the children were keen to get started. This was the day that Amy had been looking forward to ever since she saw the captivating photograph on the back of the Choco-Snaps cereal box. They jumped into the jeep and Izzy lowered the roof so they could get a great view of any wildlife that happened to be out and about this early. Izzy advised them to be on the lookout for leaves and small twigs and branches falling to earth. This was a good sign and could mean seeing monkeys, flying squirrels or large birds. George had his binoculars handy and kept his eyes peeled for any signs of activity. Amy on the other hand was intent on prising as much information as she could from Izzy on the way to the centre.

'Why do they need these centres when the rainforest is so vast?'

Izzy had wanted to let the experts answer the majority of orangutan based questions but explained that the major problem was *humans*. 'Amy, I'm sad to say it, but we cause the most problems for them by felling the trees and building roads. When the trees are cut down it makes it difficult for the orangutans to lead a normal life. These animals are arboreal, meaning they live in the trees. The more trees we cut down the harder it is for them to mate, find food or build a home.'

'Why would the local people cut down so many trees if they know it affects the orangutans so much?'

'It isn't so much the local or indigenous people. They only cut down what they need to build a house or even a small boat. Timber and palm oil are the top exports from our country. Some timber companies are not replacing the trees quickly enough and building extra roads. The worst people are those who are not allowed to cut down any trees but do it anyway. Illegal logging is a problem across Borneo. It's against the law but these people are rarely caught and punished. It's also a big problem in the Amazon rainforest.'

'I thought building roads was a good thing Izzy?' enquired Amy.

'Some roads yes, but if a road is built and it splits a rainforest into two halves then the orangutans are not likely to walk across the road to the other half. The road has divided their choice of habitat in two, making it half the size. A large portion of the rainforest has been cut down to plant oil-palm trees.' She pointed to the lines and lines of trees on one side of the road. 'The trees produce an orange coloured fruit and from that you can extract a yellowish fatty oil which you use for cooking or making soap. This is good for employing locals but not good for the animals. I'll let the keepers explain the other problem, poachers.'

Izzy looked at the palm oil plantation by the roadside and shook her head in disgust. She did not want to ruin the children's special day so left out some of the more depressing facts about these plantations. Was cooking oil, lipstick or a bar of soap worth the extinction of so many animals? The palm oil plantations had encroached into protected areas but no-one had the power to stop them. Her country would soon find out the hard way when the orangutans disappeared from the wild.

As the scenery whistled by, Amy sat quietly thinking about the many problems animals in Borneo face to survive. It was not long before they slowed to a crawl. This was the sign that greeted the children's arrival:

BORNEO
ORANGUTAN REHABILITATION
CENTRE,
SEPILOK

They were so thrilled about the prospect of seeing orangutans up close that they almost leapt from the jeep before it came to a standstill. Firstly, Izzy took them to meet the keepers, although it was quite a walk to get there. There were a number of boardwalks leading in different directions into the rainforest. Izzy led the way and eventually they came upon two men who were pleased to see her.

'Hello there, Iz,' said the first, 'you're looking very well this morning.'

'Who are your new friends Izzy?' said the other.

'Amy and George, I would like you to meet my friends Sati and Nazarus.'

'Helo, apa khabar, hopefully that meant hello, how are you?' said Amy, her cheeks going slightly pink with embarrassment.

'Selamat Pagi,' added George.

'Well done! You know more Malay than most of the tourists that come through here,' replied Sati. 'You are lucky to win the competition, normally no one is allowed near the orangutans except the keepers and Izzy. Tourists are allowed onto certain viewing platforms but cannot approach the animals. This is because humans and orangutans are so alike that it can be dangerous for them to have too much contact. The orangutans might catch a human disease and get sick making it hard to get them back into the wild.' Sati pointed at a: no smoking, no spitting and no littering sign. 'Human illnesses can be passed through their spittle and cigarette smoke is just as harmful to orangutans as it is to humans. We have a lot of responsibility for rehabilitating the orangutans here. Some even have to be taught how to feed themselves again'.

'Why do you need to teach them to feed again?' asked Amy.

'Sometimes they are injured or the mother gets sick and is unable to care for the young. The worst-case scenario would be if a poacher had killed or captured the mother. The male orangutans don't do anything for the babies, as they prefer to be on their own. The males are solitary animals.'

'Maybe someone should shoot the poachers or throw them in cages and see how they like it,' said George, incensed that anyone could be so cruel.

'We agree with you but it's difficult to catch these poachers in such a big forest. There are too few people to protect the animals. It would be like having fifty policemen to protect the whole of London. It's an incredibly dangerous job because the poachers know stealing, trafficking or killing endangered animals is a serious crime. They always carry guns and are prepared to use them because of the long jail sentences if caught. There may only be 12,000 to 20,000 orangutans left in the whole of Borneo. A hundred years ago there would have been six times that figure,' replied Nazarus.

'The other problem is the palm oil plantations. Palm oil can be used to create biofuels; it also goes into foodstuffs and soap products. Great swathes of the rainforests across both here and in Indonesia are being lost to create new land for palm oil plantations. This plan is not sustainable, our country must change but it needs to happen very quickly,' added Sati.

The children sat quietly thinking about how stupid humans could be. An awful thought whizzed across their minds. How long would it be before there were no orangutans in the wilds of Borneo's rainforests? How long before humans cut down all the trees here just so we can have cheap biscuits, soap, margarine and cosmetics?

Sati could see Amy looking a little overcast so he took her by the hand, 'We'll go and grab the buckets of fruit while the other three make their way to the feeding platform.'

When they were all together again, George enquired about the series of ropes tied half way up the tree trunks or attached to pieces of wood like telegraph poles. They led all the way from inside the rainforest to the platform where they were seated.

Nazarus explained, 'Because orangutans are arboreal animals they prefer to stay away from the forest floor where most of their predators are. Also leeches are found lower down and they don't want those bloodsuckers attached to their bodies. This system of ropes encourages the younger orangutans, who may have only recently returned to the wild, to come back for food if they are finding it difficult to fend for themselves.'

Sati told them that pregnant mothers, having left the centre years ago, often reappeared when they needed extra food. He revealed that the word orangutan came from the Malay and Indonesian words, *orang* and *hutan*. 'Orang' means person and 'hutan' means wood or forest, so that is why they are often called the 'man of the forest'.

Amy was thinking how exotic the name orangutan sounded when suddenly there was movement along the system of ropes. 'Look over there George,' Amy whispered, 'isn't she beautiful?'

'Becks is normally first to arrive for breakfast,' replied Sati.

'Is that short for Rebecca?' asked Amy.

'Oh, Becks is a boy!' answered Sati. George sniggered and got a withering stare from Amy. 'It's short for Beckham because Naz is a big Manchester United fan!'

'Get your banana ready Amy,' said George, as Becks drew closer to the platform.

Amy half-peeled the banana as Becks came swinging along the rope, one hand after another. It suddenly dawned on her why they called the metal rings in her school playground 'monkey rings'. The closer he got to the platform the more both children could see the human likeness in the eyes, ears and hands. Even the facial expressions changed regularly as he drew closer. She held out the banana as Becks slowly lowered himself off the rope and down the wooden post until he was next to her on the platform. Amy could have sworn he smiled when he looked straight at her before grasping the banana she was holding. With infinite precision he took the last of the banana peel off, dropped the skin on the platform and scoffed it down in one mouthful. Amy reached behind her for more food and Sati passed her some wild figs. Becks took these from Amy one by one and he looked content with his breakfast. He began to caress her blonde bobbed hair with one hand whilst feeding himself with the other.

'That's a sign of affection when they touch your head. It shows they are interested in you. It helps that you are their size, easier than if you were a full-grown man or woman meeting him for the first time,' said Nazarus softly.

After watching Amy and Becks for a while, George noticed the rope was vibrating. He looked along it and followed it back towards the rainforest. He was overjoyed to see a hefty female orangutan with a baby clinging tightly to her, followed by another orangutan, who was bigger than Becks.

Nazarus and Izzy crept away from the feeding platform so they could check on Jamala, a young female orangutan that Izzy had found on a trek through the rainforest. Her arm had been badly injured and currently she was unable to climb trees or swing along the rope. Izzy rarely intervened with injured animals in the rainforest. However, due to the rapidly declining numbers of orangutans in the wild, she had made a rare exception. Injured animals make easy prey for predators in any ecosystem. A clouded leopard or six metre reticulated python would have certainly made short work of Jamala.

Back on the platform George armed himself with some fruit and waited. He was nervous because the mother was the largest orangutan he had ever seen. When you look at animals in a zoo, it can be difficult to grasp how big they can really grow in the wild.

Sati saw him tense up and placed a reassuring hand on his shoulder, 'Don't worry, Britney's been coming here for years. She just wants to come and show off her baby and get some easy food. As long as you don't make any loud noises or sudden movements when she first arrives on the platform, you'll be fine.'

When Britney arrived on the platform she ambled over to George, sniffing first the fruit, then him and then the fruit, before breaking the banana in half and feeding it to her baby. Sati told him the young one was called 'Ronaldo' so he had no need to ask what sex he was or who had named him! Britney sat herself down beside George, as if she had just turned up for Sunday lunch. Britney took the wild figs and George observed her crinkled skin, human eyes and dextrous hands, as well as her lovely, orangey-red hair. He was astounded by the range of facial expressions that she was capable of. It was now obvious to see just how closely related humans are to orangutans. George could not help his thoughts from wandering as he gazed into Britney's eyes; who would want to harm or kill these magnificent primates? Why do humans always end up destroying the habitats of so much wildlife? What would it be like to face a full-grown, muscular, male orangutan? Suddenly Amy's Dad Tom popped into his head, with his reddish ginger hair, huge arm span and gigantic chest. Tom often picked them both up with ease at Cuckoo Lane barbecues. George liked Tom but thought that he might not take kindly to being compared to the mighty 'man of the forest'.

Anyone who set eyes upon the children that morning would have thought they were just like *Mowgli* from the *Jungle Book* and had been brought up in the wild. Sati was sitting behind them feeding Fergie, the last orangutan to turn up. Each orangutan wanted to touch and smell both the children, much to their delight. This was the experience of a lifetime, an unforgettable day that would stay with them forever. When the orangutans had eaten their fill they rose slowly, clambered up the pole and swung back along the rope into the rainforest.

Amy and George were elated but speechless; they stretched out and sat back while Sati talked. He explained that not every orangutan came back out the forest for feeding time. This was a positive sign because it showed they were rehabilitated and finding their own food in the wild. Often orangutans that had recovered to full health at the centre had been taken elsewhere in Borneo. A helicopter had flown some to remote parts of the rainforest to start a new life. Amy raised her eyebrows in astonishment, but Sati explained that the orangutans were sedated for the journey to avoid distress. Orangutans that had been kept in captivity for long periods were the most difficult to rehabilitate.

He narrated the true story of a children's television programme in Taiwan in the 1980's. The star of the show was a beautiful young orangutan called Shylie. Due to the TV show there was a surge in demand as Taiwanese people wanted orangutans as household pets. A large number were illegally smuggled from Borneo to Taiwan. The adult orangutans were often killed and the young sold for thousands of dollars. As the primates grew, people quickly realised that an orangutan did not make a good house pet. These people often did not understand the cruelty of captivity but instead foolishly thought they were giving the orangutans a good home. Only about one fifth of the thousand young orangutans that were smuggled into Taiwan survived.

The orangutans had swung out of sight; so a sudden rustling in the bushes all around them startled the children. Amy and George had heard of strong winds and torrential storms dropping inches of rain in minutes. Monsoons are commonplace in Asia; the seasonal strong winds bring huge amounts of rainfall that can turn roads into rivers, wash away homes and ultimately cost many lives. The noise level rose but no wind screeched like that. They became fearful it was predators waiting to pounce on an orangutan or even them. It was coming from the bushes beneath the feeding platform. Encircled by noise, the forest was acting as a cloak of secrecy for whatever was right beneath them. The children found it difficult to describe the cacophony of noise they heard. A mixture of bawling, cackling, claps, cries, howls, slurps, slaps and whoops.

It happened so quickly that they did not know what to do or have time to react. Furry arms, gangly legs and sharp teeth surrounded them. Simultaneously they appeared from above and below the platform. Out of the forest came an entire troop of long-tailed macaques, now swarming amongst them.

'Gadzooks!' shouted George.

'They've scratched me!' shrieked Amy.

'Mind your teeth fur-ball' shouted George, as he narrowly avoided being bitten by dropping the food in his hand.

They wanted to bolt from the platform but were swamped by monkeys. The frenzy of activity even made Sati jump. He was used to seeing six, maybe eight turn up to pick over the leftovers, not an entire troop of twenty-five or thirty. A macaque was perched on Amy's shoulder and another was on George's head. Sati shooed these off and slowly but surely lead them off the feeding platform until they were a safe distance away. After George's initial shock had subsided, he questioned why they had to leave the feeding platform. The monkeys may have had sharp teeth and claws but they appeared playful from this distance.

'Watch what happens when the larger macaques are full and the scraps begin to run out. I've never seen so many here in all my years at the centre. Remarkable!' said Sati.

The rumpus was deafening, as the macaques became more excitable and then bad-tempered as the food ran out. There were now brawls between macaques all over the platform and Sati was right, even the small ones looked menacing. George had been listening closely to the macaques. He thought this was a good time to learn how to imitate them, as they were too busy fighting to take any notice. Sati showed George how to mimic the calls he knew. The monkeys were still squabbling over scraps so paid no attention to George as he practised.

Amy had retrieved her camera and was taking photographs of the long-tailed macaques whilst all this unfolded. After the scraps on the rainforest floor and on the platform had been cleared, a loud call went up from one of the large males. Just as suddenly as they came they vanished back into the rainforest.

Sati was at a loss to explain the strange incident. 'These long-tailed macaques rarely move away from their own territory. They stay by the river so they can sleep in branches overhanging the water. It's safer there from predators like monitor lizards and snakes. Something must have happened for them to have uprooted and changed their daily routine.'

'What routine do they have?' asked Amy.

'They go foraging for food in the morning and then return to base for a break. During that time they groom themselves or each other, sleep and play. They forage for food later in the afternoon and return home before the predators become more active at dusk. Finally, they enjoy a little more playtime before climbing the trees to sleep.'

'Apart from the predator part, those monkeys have a first-class lifestyle. Lots of time for sleeping, playing and eating. That sounds good to me!' exclaimed George.

Amy was more concerned as to why a whole troop of monkeys had left its home. Her mind was racing and her brain ached. So much had happened since they woke up that morning. She had fulfilled her dream to feed the orangutans but other issues kept nagging away at her. The children had not realised how much time had already passed.

Sati showed them to a dining room for a late lunch and left them while he went to find Izzy and Nazarus. Amy took out her drawing pad and George wrote in his journal, content to make their notes and sketches while it was still fresh in their minds. They knew their parents would be intrigued to know all that had happened on this holiday. When Izzy returned with the two keepers, they had their hands full with trays of food. On the menu today was: sweet and sour chicken, homemade vegetable soup, rice, bean sprouts in a tangy sauce and an assortment of fruit.

'I heard about those mischievous monkeys. You have to be careful. I've seen them steal bags, sunglasses, cameras, hats and all sorts over the years. Many people across Borneo rely on those monkeys for their livelihood. The monkeys are trained to go up trees, twist off the coconuts and throw them to the ground. Clever macaques, eh?' asked Izzy.

The children nodded in agreement. They chatted away merrily for the next few hours, asking questions and discussing the local wildlife.

The time came when Izzy had to tell the children that they had better leave and let Sati and Nazarus get back to work. The keepers disappeared briefly and came back with two bags filled with T-shirts, fact sheets, postcards, stickers, pictures and lots of other paraphernalia. Sati and Nazarus were sad to see the lively Amy and George go; it was great to have young ones around who were so interested in the local wildlife.

'Selamat Tingal, terima kasih,' 'goodbye, thank you,' the children shouted whilst waving energetically from the back seat of the jeep.

On the drive back to the lodge the children were chattering away. Izzy sat back in the driver's seat and nodded when necessary; delighted that they were in such high spirits. The journey passed in a flash with talk of their favourite orangutans, the amiable keepers and the crazy macaque monkeys. When they arrived back at the lodge they got cleaned up, had a light dinner together before playing a few games of cards. When you are in a foreign land and have activities planned from dawn till dusk, it is amazing how tired you get. Amy and George were completely drained by the time they went to bed, again much earlier than they would have done back home. They barely chatted for five minutes before their eyelids became heavy and they drifted off to sleep. That night they had splendid dreams overflowing with wild animals, hairy mammals and exciting new adventures.

CHAPTER FIVE

The next morning Izzy woke them up for a breakfast consisting of fruit, toast and orange juice. She told them more about where they were going to visit that day. Gomantong Caves were famous because they housed tens of thousands of birds. This in itself would not be that surprising, as many caves housed many birds. The surprise would be that the birds' nests were harvested and used to make a popular soup.

Amy was astonished because she thought birds' nest soup was a joke to describe bad cooking or a dish that looked terrible. She found it hard to believe that anyone would actually pay to eat this ghastly sounding soup. Izzy tried not to tell them too much, as there were things today that were best not discussed over breakfast. George was not thrilled when he heard they would be visiting a cave, although he kept this to himself. He was still tired from the previous day's activities. He was not really a morning person and his family would vouch for that.

They soon set off for the Gomantong caves because it was a long journey by road. The children weren't sure these dirt tracks should be called a road. George thought it was more suitable for rally cars. By the time they arrived at the trail, which led to the caves, their stomachs felt as though they had come off a rough ferry crossing. Izzy had driven the jeep as slowly as she could but some of the potholes were so large they could have swallowed a smaller vehicle.

'Wowzers, I never thought I'd have jet lag and motion sickness at the same time,' said George queasily.

'If you are going to throw up, please do it away from me,' said Amy rather unsympathetically.

They sat down on some rocks to put on their leech socks and let their stomachs settle. The day was scorching and it would get more humid on the walk through the rainforest. Izzy was pleased they had remembered their water bottles and waterproof jackets. She had explained the importance of drinking water regularly. Humans sweat more when it is hot because the body has to work harder to cool itself down. To avoid dehydration you must constantly replace this lost water. The consequences of not doing so included exhaustion, nausea, headaches, vomiting, fainting and a rapid change in body temperature. Even though it meant carrying a heavier daypack the children were keen to avoid the dangers of dehydrating.

Amy and George had questioned the need to bring their cagoules when it was a brilliant day with crystal blue skies and not the faintest breeze. Izzy asked them to trust her and wait and see. They felt perkier after their rest and began the trek to the caves.

Izzy gave them a final warning, 'You must keep your eyes peeled because it's a popular spot with reptiles, particularly snakes. Poisonous snakes are seen along here, especially the mangrove viper and the green tree viper. There's lots of food for snakes here like rodents, birds and frogs. Snakes are masters of disguise and blend in with their surroundings. Their camouflage helps them to catch their prey but it makes it much more difficult for you to see them!'

George stepped forward, bowed his head down and gestured them forward, saying in a mock posh voice, 'Ladies first, after you please.'

'I think it best if I do go first, thank you George,' replied Izzy with a wry smile.

Even though Amy was fond of snakes she was glad to see Izzy lead the way. They continued through the rainforest before arriving at a slow moving stream. To get across it there was a makeshift bamboo bridge, which did not look as if it could take the weight of a small child, let alone an adult. The stream was shallow and appealing enough that they could have taken off their leech socks and waded through it. Izzy went first, closely followed by Amy, then George whose mind was elsewhere. He was looking upwards for any sign of venomous snakes in the low branches. There are times for daydreaming and there are times for snake spotting but not when crossing a rickety bridge, however small. Seconds later there was a splash and an 'Ow!'

George's foot had gone straight through the old bridge giving him a sore knee and a wet foot. Amy giggled and eventually offered him a hand but soon stopped dead in her tracks.

'Look behind you! Follow the ripples. Can you see them?' she whispered, pointing upstream. He thought it was a pantomime joke but like a bolt from the blue he realised she was not kidding.

'Don't just stand there admiring them, help me out of here!'

'Be careful not to disturb them children, this is their home,' admonished Izzy.

'Disturb *them*, I don't want them to disturb *me*,' protested George innocently.

Amy helped George up whilst keeping an eye on the snakes moving silently through the water towards them.

'Baby reticulated pythons, probably out hunting for frogs. They are good swimmers and can grow to six or seven metres in length. They coil their bodies around their prey, then squeeze and squeeze until it can't breathe. Then they dislocate their jaw and eat it whole.'

George stopped complaining about his wet foot and stood admiring the snakes, varying in length from sixty to ninety centimetres. Once the pythons had swum out of sight, the young explorers began moving again so Izzy continued, 'The adult pythons can eat wild boars, deer and monkeys! In fact, anything they can get their coils around. Once a python has had a substantial meal it can take over a week to digest it. It won't need to eat for a few weeks or even as long as a month,' replied Izzy.

En route to the caves, George tried to picture what amount of food these young snakes would have to eat to get ten or twelve times bigger. He marvelled that any snake could eat a deer or a monkey whole; the snakes jaw must dislocate really far apart to be able to do that. He weighed less than a deer so never wanted to come across a snake of that size. Putting aside all thoughts of being digested inside a python's belly, he jogged to catch up with the others.

Onwards through the rainforest they went until they came to the gigantic cave. The tiny swiftlets were not easily identifiable but there were thousands of tiny black dots darting in and out of the cave entrance. A cool, refreshing breeze brought something unexpected with it.

Amy posed the most pressing question, 'Oh Izzy, what on earth is that awful smell?'

'I'm sorry to tell you but that's as good as the smell gets for the next few hours. The closer we get the stronger the smell of guano is!'

'But what is guano?' asked George, forever curious.

'There's no nice way to put this. With thousands of birds and over a million bats living in one cave, a lot of poo is produced and the smell can be overpowering. They cannot clear it up because the pungent smell attracts the birds back to nest here each year. You get used to the smell after a while, or so I'm told by the workers,' Izzy explained.

'Amy, could you honestly work with this smell everyday?' asked George.

'I don't know. If there were no other jobs around or I needed money then I might. Are the birds nests expensive Izzy?'

'There are two types of nest and both are expensive. One is more valuable than the other. White nests are made from one thing – birds' saliva. They are much more valuable. Black nests are made from feathers and saliva. The black nests are cheaper because they are more common inside the cave.'

Amy and George gazed at Izzy in disbelief.

'Who in the world pays money for the worst soup combination ever? Beef and veg, okay, chicken and sweet corn, fine, lentil and bacon, acceptable but I draw the line at bird feather and saliva soup,' exclaimed George.

'The Chinese consider birds-nest soup a rare delicacy, a real treat. They believe that it's good for your skin and liver, amongst other things. The Chinese are masters of old medicine, especially when using plants and herbs so it could be true. One kilogram of white birds nests can sell for 5000 Malaysian Ringgit or around $1250 US dollars. The black nests sell for between $450 and $550 but prices frequently change. When there was a shortage across Borneo, the price rose sharply and it cost the same as silver.'

Silence greeted Izzy, as they had no comment to this astonishing fact. They just stood admiring the cave thinking about how much money was inside a cave of this magnitude. Izzy let them ponder all this for a while. She smiled to herself because the children were finding out firsthand that fact was often stranger than fiction.

'I think it's time we put on our raincoats and took a closer look,' said Izzy.

The light-bulbs above their heads were blinking as Amy and George finally realised why they needed raincoats. With that much bird poo raining down, they wished they had brought umbrellas! They followed Izzy towards the cave entrance with their flashlights and torches to hand. As they drew closer, the guano smell became so intense their eyes watered. A wooden boardwalk led directly into the cave and saved any visitors from walking knee deep in guano. The further they went in the darker it became.

'The floor of the cave is moving, it's rippling like the sea.' Using her torch, Amy inspected it closer and let out a gasp of horror, 'George! Look at that. There are thousands of them, a giant swarm of them!'

George stared down into the seething mass of insects which made him feel sick all over again. If there was one thing George hated, it was cockroaches.

'Sorry to correct you Amy but it's a swarm of ants or bees and an 'intrusion' of cockroaches,' said Izzy.

At that moment in time, George could not have cared less what they were called. He was trying hard not to throw up.

'Guano is a delicacy for cockroaches and attracts tens of thousands of them. This perfect habitat means they keep breeding until they create a sea of cockroaches. This is a rare sight,' explained Izzy, who always marvelled at the spectacle. It took the children time to get used to what was lurking beneath the boardwalk.

The noise grew and grew the deeper inside they went. The twittering of the birds echoed throughout the cavernous cave. It was difficult for them to tell the difference between the small swifts and the bats. Their knowledgeable guide informed them that even though it was dark in the caves, the bats became more active when night approached or early in the morning. Therefore, most of the movement during the day would be the swifts.

Amy and George encountered other startling creatures inside the cave including numerous insects and spiders. As they shone their spotlight on a large spider, it would scurry off into the darkness. The centipedes were as large as any in the insect house at London Zoo.

'How come the spiders and centipedes get so big in here, Izzy?' asked Amy.

'Their main food is cockroaches so they never go short and don't have to travel far for lunch.'

They continued round the boardwalk but as George stopped to brush bird poo from his shoulder, he caught a glimpse of something odd, 'Come over here, look at this phantom!'

Amy shone her light on it and saw a cockroach, white from top to bottom.

'It looks ghostly doesn't it? It's an albino cockroach; you get albino humans, animals, plants and insects. It means they are lacking the pigment that makes their skin the usual colour,' said Izzy.

There was more in this cave than they had bargained for. One question had them both stumped. How on earth did they harvest the nests when they were so high up in the cave? Izzy had this in hand. Once outside, they removed their poo covered jackets and she led them towards a small hut. A venerable old man saw them coming and waved from the veranda.

'Hello Izzy,' he shouted, 'Bring your young friends over.'

After climbing up the wooden steps to the veranda she introduced them, 'Amy, George, meet Jamji. He looks after the cave, the nests and the young men who harvest them.'

'Selamat Petang,' said the youngsters.

'Come, sit and drink.' They sat on rickety wooden chairs on the veranda while Jamji went inside to get drinks. A few minutes later he came out holding a tray with homemade lemonade on it, 'Any questions you have, ask?'

'How do you get to the nests that are high up in the cave and do you still collect them?' asked Amy.

'I'm long past my climbing days. I leave climbing up and down ladders to young men. First, we must make offerings to spirit of cave. We leave fruit and burn incense. Then we pray that we be safe and have good harvest. Male birds build during the breeding season, which is only a month long. It's a dangerous job climbing long, thin rattan or bamboo ladders. I've photos inside, so you see for yourself.' He got up and tottered inside. The homemade lemonade was dreadful, so sour that every sip was like having a mouthful of fizzy cola bottles. He brought out photographs and a small section of an old ladder. When they looked through the photographs and examined the ladder, it did not seem possible that anyone could climb it. It looked thin, frayed, homemade and very unsafe. George prided himself on his climbing ability but he would never have attempted to climb one. It had to be, without doubt, one of the most perilous jobs in the world.

'Where are the safety harnesses and support ropes?' enquired George.

'Sometimes they have extra bamboo scaffolding but no safety harness. Just cave spirit and me to protect them. That's why they do as I say! If they break rules then there is chance they die, I tell them work in pairs, act with respect, pray to cave spirit and they survive, simple. Workers sometimes die in other caves but *not* mine. The deaths are because the workers fool around,' said Jamji gravely.

They handled samples of the different types of birds' nests; one white and the other looked more blood red than black. He cooked up a small amount, enough for a few mouthfuls each. He had soaked the nest for hours beforehand so it did not take long to cook. It was sticky and gooey, more like jelly than soup. It was much better than they expected and actually quite sweet. They spent time talking with the old man but had no chance to throw away the super sour lemonade. Eventually, they downed what was left and thanked him for the birds nest soup. They wished him a good harvest and waved goodbye as they headed across the clearing back into the rainforest.

When they reached the jeep Amy turned to George, 'I could never ever work there, I'd be too scared to climb the ladders and scaffolding, I don't really like cockroaches and the smell would drive me crazy!'

George nodded in complete agreement with his friend. One visit was enough for him to realise how lucky they were. Neither had been looking forward to the journey home but at least they had a lot to talk about to take their minds off the bumpy dirt track. They had seen pythons and visited the malodorous, colossal cave filled with a sea of cockroaches, bats, birds, whopping centipedes and giant spiders.

When they arrived back at the lodge, Izzy had some jobs to do. She let them help prepare dinner and then entertain themselves for a while. They had a simple dinner together but Izzy could see they were exhausted.

Getting used to the time difference was taking its toll on them both. Tomorrow, she would take them on a relaxing boat trip to spot wildlife and then organise activities closer to the lodge. She excused herself saying she too would like an early night. This gave Amy and George the chance to saunter off to their room and get some well-earned sleep.

CHAPTER SIX

George raised one eyelid, then the other. Not instantly recognising his surroundings increased the uneasy feeling inside him. It was dark but he could just make out what must be Amy hidden underneath her blankets and mosquito net. He looked for his torch but it was nowhere to be found. A scratching noise was coming from somewhere inside the room. When his eyes became accustomed to the gloom, he checked around his bed but found nothing. He did not want to get right out of bed; no slippers, no carpet and the floor was bound to be cold.

The scratching continued to get worse, so George dragged himself from underneath his warm blanket. How could Amy not hear it? Come to think of it, she could probably sleep through an earthquake! Her blanket was pulled up, fully covering her head. George saw her blanket moving ever so slightly, so he lifted her mosquito net and edged back her blanket. He let out a muffled scream, her bed was overrun with dirty brown cockroaches, some took flight, he swatted at them, their prickly legs on his hands, now his arms, in his hair, on his face....

'George, George, shhh, you're having a nightmare! It's me,' soothed Amy.

He came round like a punch drunk boxer, sweating and not knowing which way was up. George's dreams had been filled with dark places and crawling with an intrusion of cockroaches. He was clearly not himself over breakfast, so Amy quietly reassured Izzy that he would be fine once he had some food inside him and had woken up properly.

'My plan is to go out on my boat in search of animals along the Kinabatangan River. The river is 560 kilometres long and home to Pygmy elephants, orangutans, hundreds of species of birds and huge lizards to name but a few. Its most famous resident is an exceptionally rare primate, in fact a truly extraordinary monkey.' The children pricked up their ears.

'What rare monkey?' enquired Amy.

'What's so remarkable about it?' asked George simultaneously.

Izzy continued, 'It can only be found in a handful of places across Borneo and has some distinctive features. It's called the proboscis monkey because the male has a long pendulous nose. So a proboscis is a long nose, snout or even an elephant's trunk.'

Amy briefly interrupted to ask what pendulous meant. If she never asked or checked words, how could she improve her vocabulary?

'It means dangling or something that's hanging down, like the pendulum inside a clock. When you see the male monkey's massive nose swinging free, you'll understand. The nose is so large it often hangs over its mouth. The female's nose is much more petite. It's also called the 'long-nosed' monkey but the people of Borneo call it the 'Dutch Monkey'. Hundreds of years ago when the first traders came from Holland on ships, the natives thought the monkey was the spitting image of the Dutch seamen. With their big noses, fat bellies, hairy appearance and their sunburnt shoulders resembling the reddish brown haired monkeys.'

'They sound superb but shouldn't we get going?' suggested George excitedly.

'Not so fast, you need hats, sun-cream and water. There's no shelter on the boat so it gets hot out there. It might also be worth taking your notebooks and sketchpads. I've a cool box for sandwiches and fruit. I'll get my things and meet you outside in five minutes. Don't forget your binoculars!'

The children scurried off to get everything packed. In five minutes flat they were ready to rock. With their hats and sunglasses on, they felt pretty cool and ready for action.

Izzy stepped into the boat and George handed her the supplies. She had previously asked them if they could swim and tread water, to which she had received a resounding '*yes*'.

'I know by now that you're sensible, so I won't insist on you wearing your lifejackets. We won't be travelling fast and the water couldn't be calmer. Also, we may not come across another boat all day. Those lifejackets get hot and sweaty but they make excellent seat cushions, certainly better than hard wooden benches.' Izzy flicked a switch and the small propeller engine began to tick over. One twist of the throttle and they were off.

Amy noticed two small paddles under the seats, 'Do you expect us to breakdown, Izzy?'

'No, this engine is old but it hasn't broken down on me yet. The paddles are here because I don't want to scare the animals when we get close to them. We can use the paddles instead of the engine. If you need to draw something, I can hold us in position with a paddle. Most of the animals here are naturally shy, scared of natural predators and humans.'

Surrounded by wildlife, Amy soon pointed out a well-built bird seen through her binoculars.

'Our first raptor of the day,' said Izzy. Amy and George laughed, as they really enjoyed those blockbuster dinosaur movies. Naturally they wondered what Izzy really meant to say.

Izzy had no idea what they found funny, so carried on, 'It's a fish eagle, a bird of prey. They include hawks, eagles, buzzards, kites and even condors. All these fierce predator birds are called 'raptors'. They swoop down and snatch their prey with razor sharp talons or their beak.' It was as if the eagle heard them as it hurtled towards the surface of the river at breakneck speed. It soon went out of sight so Izzy turned the throttle and they motored downriver to get a better view. When they caught sight of it again, it was obvious why the eagle had fired itself downwards. It had a good size fish between its talons and was flying away.

'That eagle burst out of the sky like a comet and bagged its breakfast!' remarked George.

They noticed a host of other birds appearing, birds that had more sense than to come out when an eagle was in the neighbourhood. Tiny kingfishers clothed in majestic colours from beak to tail; flashes of purple, orange and scarlet, others were green and black with blue stripes. There were stork-billed kingfishers which had larger bright red beaks with flecks of yellowy orange at the front with indigo and green wings. They knew they were somewhere special when they came across an unusual pigeon. Not your common 'rat with wings' English pigeon, this bird looked handsome with its iridescent coat, blue green wings and white and grey patterned breast. They never thought a pigeon would impress them so much.

Izzy slowed the boat next to a drifting log. A bird had perched on it, dipping its beak in and out of the water in a peculiar fashion. 'This is an egret, part of the heron family. They eat crustaceans like crabs but prefer to hunt for small fish from logs or in the shallow water.' The egret's head darted down, shooting its sharp beak into the water and skewering a fish. It raised its head up and with one flick of the neck, the fish had gone from the end of the beak into the air before being swallowed - it did this manoeuvre with some style.

'Wow, that's the cat's meow!' exclaimed George, 'We have breakfast and then get to watch everything else hunt for theirs.'

'That sharp beak looks like a handy tool for fishing,' added Amy.

'This is an incredible place to see such a variety of birds, monkeys and other wildlife living in their natural habitat. This is the only place in the world where all eight types of hornbills can be seen. I am surprised we haven't come across a single proboscis monkey yet. We should carry on along the river because there are some breeding sites that they use every year.'

'How many years have you been working here?' asked Amy.

'I'm not sure but many, many years. Borneo is my country and I love animals, so I'll carry on until I'm old and grey.'

'I can't think of many jobs better than yours Izzy, except maybe owning my own football club or being a stuntman,' commented George truthfully.

They continued on their trip until Amy heard rustling in the trees and saw branches vibrating. This was it! Was it to be a first sighting of a long-nosed monkey? Amy was more excited than when waiting for the orangutans to arrive. It was the exhilaration, the anticipation and most of all, not knowing what to expect that gave her butterflies. She had never even seen a picture of this legendary monkey.

A small monkey zipped from a tree and perched on a branch close to the boat. It had spiky hair coming from all sides of its pink and black face, a long tail and light orange brown fur.

'That monkey looks like it's had a fight with a hairdryer, and lost!' whispered George.

'Or had a serious electric shock,' quipped Amy, before pointing out that it did not have any features of a long-nosed monkey, except maybe its tail.

'That's a silver leaf langur. Its furry coat has silver tips. In a certain light it shimmers like silver as it moves through the trees. They are very inquisitive when young,' advised Izzy.

She switched off the outboard motor and Amy sat sketching the monkey, while George took photos and made a few notes on its appearance. They needed photographs to show their younger siblings, Bethany and Vincent. They would be entranced by the monkey's mad hairdo. The children were pleased to see their first primate of the day; except for each other because the primate family includes orangutans, monkeys, great apes and humans.

They meandered along the river and Izzy explained the call of the male proboscis monkey. Its call came mainly through the immense nose and sounded like 'kee-honk'. Amy tried a few times but Izzy thought it better if she held her nose whilst making the call. This worked well and within no time at all, Izzy thought both of them sounded just like these unusual monkeys. The boat drew up next to a popular area where the proboscis monkeys liked to hang out. Their guide was sure they would see them here because it was a regular breeding ground and there was a good supply of fruits, flowers, seeds and leaves.

For quite some time they took turns making 'kee-honk' calls. There was not a creak of a branch or the rustle of a leaf, except that caused by the calming wind. Long after Izzy and Amy had given up, George continued to call these mysterious monkeys. He loved to mimic animals and he was desperate to see one of these big nosed, pot-bellied monkeys in the flesh.

'I don't know where they can be! This has never happened before,' reported Izzy anxiously as she scanned the tree line with her binoculars.

Amy could hear the concern in her voice and even though she was no expert on the subject and had no idea where they were, she said, 'Maybe it's just too hot for them today. Who would be out basking in this heat?'

'You may be right but this is one of the remarkable facts about them. They are one of the few monkeys that enjoy swimming. When it gets too hot or they get frightened, they jump in the water. Let's go and try one of their bathing spots next,' replied Izzy rather unconvincingly.

George burst in, 'I think I know the reason why they are not swimming around here today. I spy a crocodile, look!'

Amy gripped the side of the boat until her knuckles were white.

Izzy took a few light strokes with the paddle to get the boat into a better position. As they went closer to the log-like creature Izzy said, 'Look closer at the head, then you will see what it is.'

On cue the animal turned its head towards the boat and rudely stuck out its forked tongue.

'It's a giant lizard!' blurted Amy in surprise. She was still edgy but not as nervous as when it had been a crocodile.

'You spotted a monitor lizard and a large one at that. They grow to around two and a half metres; this is a prize specimen. It's about two metres from the tip of the nose to the end of the tail. A lizard this size could eat birds, fish, pigs, rodents, monkeys if it could catch them and any injured animals it came across,' said Izzy.

Amy and George took plenty of photos because their friends would never believe they had seen this monster. The lizard flicked its tail and effortlessly glided towards the riverbank. It pulled itself out of the water, the children gasped now its full size was revealed.

'This lizard must weigh maybe fifteen to seventeen kilograms. It's a relation of the Komodo dragon. The main difference is that the Komodo dragon grows to just over three metres in length and it weighs much, much more. The heaviest recorded Komodo dragon weighed around 160 kilograms, which means nine or ten times the bodyweight of this big lizard. These reptiles use their powerful muscular tails as whips against prey,' said Izzy.

'The way it walks makes it look like a plodding dinosaur,' replied George. The children found it difficult to comprehend that any lizard could weigh so much more than this well-built reptile.

'I'm glad you mentioned that George, because scientists believe Komodo dragons and crocodiles are some of the dinosaurs oldest relatives. Just like crocodiles, they have not changed for tens of thousands of years,' remarked Izzy. As the monitor lizard trudged away, not bothered in the slightest by the spectators in the boat, the children sat mesmerized. They were not disappointed that it was not a crocodile and fascinated by tales of even bigger lizards than this one. Maybe one day they would come face to face with a Komodo dragon.

Izzy switched the motor back on and they cruised away in search of the long-nosed monkeys' favourite bathing spot or at least one without two metres of lizard in it. When they got close-by, she steered the boat towards the bank and switched the engine off. She handed George a paddle and they slowly and quietly paddled round the corner so as not to startle the monkeys. Izzy aimed for a large tree trunk that was half submerged in the water. She tied the boat up and moved to the front. Before searching for the monkeys she handed out sandwiches, fruit and drinks. They had been too busy enjoying themselves to remember lunch. Amy and George tucked into their lunch in silence, enjoying the ambient noise. Meanwhile, Izzy scoured the area worriedly with her binoculars. She could hear many different bird songs, the flowing river and the water lapping against the side of the boat but, alas, no monkey calls.

Surrounded by an array of wonderful sounds and beautiful scenery, the children were preoccupied. So engrossed were they in these fantastic surroundings they had not noticed that Izzy's lunch was untouched. She looked more concerned by the minute.

After some time George piped up, 'Aren't you hungry Izzy? You should eat something as it's been hours since breakfast.'

'You two can share mine; I don't have much of an appetite.'

'Still no sign of the long-nosed monkeys, Izzy? Do you want us to try our 'kee-honk' calls?' asked Amy.

'I can't explain it! They are always along this river and we've visited their favourite sites. None in the trees, none swimming and we haven't heard a single male call or any answer to our calls. We should have seen thirty or forty of them by now,' said Izzy looking quite downhearted. Amy and George were sad to see Izzy so unhappy because they knew how much she cared about the local wildlife. They began to try their monkey calls but to no avail. George spotted a black snake with yellow rings basking in the tree and thought it might be a combination of the snakes and lizards that had driven the monkeys away from their natural habitat. Izzy explained that these particular mangrove snakes enjoyed a diet of mainly rodents and had no interest in feeding on monkeys but she was grateful for their suggestions.

After a few more hours, Izzy decided it was time to head back to the lodge. She switched on the engine and began to motor back down the river. About half way home they stopped the boat because Amy was positive she had seen movement in the bushes; it turned out to be a small family of macaque monkeys dashing in and out of the branches. The macaques, with their beards and long tails, reminded Amy of something Sati had said yesterday.

'Don't you think it's odd that you and Sati have come across something that's not quite right? Sati said he'd never seen an entire troop of macaques on the move and now you've had no sightings of the long-nosed monkeys. It might not be connected but it's rather weird, don't you think?' queried Amy. Izzy contemplated over what Amy had said before replying.

'You may have a point but I really don't know what's going on. I'll have to give it some more thought later on. I think we should have a nice relaxing day closer to the lodge tomorrow. We can put the trip to camp the night in another cave off for a few days. I think we could all do with a rest tomorrow.'

Although the children would not admit it, they could both do with a lie in. Being out in the fresh air all day, rising with the sun and daily activities were beginning to take their toll.

'We can try and find more insects and animals by the lodge. Then, if you both feel refreshed we could possibly have a quick monkey search later in the day. See if any turn up tomorrow,' reflected Izzy.

'Do you mean that we might take the boat to look for them tomorrow?' asked George.

'Yes, but only if you both feel up to it,' answered Izzy.

George thought for a minute and hesitantly asked, 'If we go out on the boat and if it's calm and if no-one's around to see a minor operating the boat....'

'There are a lot of 'ifs' in that question George,' joked Amy.

'Well, what I'm trying to say is, could you please, please show me how to operate the boat tomorrow?'

'If we go out on the boat and if it's calm, of course I can show you how to work it. My father showed me how to use an outboard motor when I was your age so I don't see any harm in it, as long as you're sensible.'

George clapped his hands together at her answer and was smiling all the way back. His disappointment at not seeing the long-nosed monkeys had been outweighed by his joy over the possibility of being a boat captain.

When they arrived back at the lodge they thanked Izzy for an excellent day. They were certain these monkeys would turn up and they had still seen raptors, birds, snakes, other monkeys and a monitor lizard, amongst other things. Amy tried to reassure Izzy that it had still been a truly memorable day along the Kinabatangan River. The children and Izzy separated until teatime, to get washed and changed. It gave them a chance to have a quick lie down before dinner. Amy and George had never shared a room before so being able to talk to your best friend the whole time was a real bonus.

Over dinner, Izzy told them that she would try to mend her old two-way CB radio so that she could communicate with other local colleagues. She had already tried to telephone some rangers and the keepers at the orangutan rehabilitation centre. Most of her friends worked outdoors and either did not own a phone, had no signal on their mobiles or never answered the indoor telephone. She was wondering if her friends had seen or heard anything of the long-nosed monkeys. Amy and George did not mind because they could play cards together and write their journals until late knowing they could stay in bed tomorrow for a good while longer.

That evening flew by and the children talked and told each other silly jokes and stories. Although it did not seem like it, they both missed their parents very much. They were having a great time, learning lots of cool stuff and enjoying a once in a lifetime experience but they were still two twelve-year-old children in a foreign country, thousands of miles away from their parents. Luckily they had each other for support, so whenever they did miss their parents, they could talk about it together knowing the other felt the same way. They had not been away a week yet but the time was galloping by. The holiday would be over in what felt like a day, the days were passing in an hour and the hours flashed by in a minute. They fell asleep before midnight exhausted but happy and safe in the knowledge that tomorrow would be another unforgettable day in Borneo.

CHAPTER SEVEN

The sun rose but the children did not. Amy and George tried to sleep in but could not due to the growing clamour outside. The early morning rumpus made by the local wildlife brought the rainforest to life each day. Countless birds did not just tweet and twitter; they chirped and chirruped; whistled and warbled; shrieked and squawked. Considering what a gorgeous morning it was, the majority were probably mating calls between love-struck birds. It was easy to start the day in a good mood with the birds' chorus wafting on the air. It was as if the birds were singing solely for them. Nature's own alarm clock consisting of a choir of thousands.

Having got washed and changed, they headed for the kitchen and prepared themselves a simple but scrumptious breakfast. They expected to see Izzy but she must have been in a different part of the lodge. After washing up they took their books to the veranda to wait for her. Amy was reading the *Jules Verne* novel '*Around the World in 80 Days*'. George's current book was *'The Hobbit' by J R R Tolkien*, as he loved reading fantasy books and had only recently finished the *Harry Potter* series. They sat reading for a while but their attention kept being drawn to the wonderful scenery encircling them: the wildlife, the flowers and the mighty trees that had stood for hundreds of years. Normally both children could sit quietly and read, even when their siblings were banging around the house like elephants. However, the scenery felt alive to them. When branches shook they would check to see if it was the wind or some monkeys coming to say hello. A distraction so beautiful and vivid would sidetrack the most avid reader.

They felt lucky to have the opportunity to discover the flora and fauna of a new country. Learning in a classroom is one thing but learning from new experiences, adventures and knowledgeable guides was completely different. Amy and George did not have to take tests or sit exams on any of this stuff; they wanted to learn because it was fun.

Izzy appeared flashing her customary smile, 'I'm sorry for keeping you waiting but I thought you'd be sleeping for a few more hours yet. I finally got the CB radio working and contacted some friends from around the region.'

'No problem, we've enjoyed chilling out and reading. I do have a quick question. I was too tired to ask what a CB radio was last night but now I'm intrigued,' George replied.

'CB stands for Citizen Band. It's a two-way radio frequency band which can be used by people to communicate with each other. I've got a small base unit with a microphone attached to it and when I use the CB radio I have a call sign, a CB nickname. My call sign is River Guide for obvious reasons. This used to be modern technology before telephones, faxes and the internet came along,' replied Izzy.

'Did your friends have any ideas? Had they seen or heard anything that might help us to solve the mystery of the missing monkeys?' added Amy.

'No clues. Most of the guides have been visiting family. When there's not much work around they go back to their hometowns. The ranger said he'd heard of two locals who'd not been seen at work since the day I picked you up, but locals are forever changing from one palm oil plantation to another,' remarked Izzy.

'Maybe we'll see some long-nosed monkeys on the boat today and that'll solve the mystery once and for all,' said George mischievously, only thinking about piloting the boat and not really about solving the primate puzzle.

Izzy smiled and after a short but deliberate pause she replied, 'Only if you are both feeling fit, healthy and refreshed after our walk. Then, maybe we can teach old Captain George the seaman how to pilot my boat.' George tried not to let on that he was ecstatic but his big smirk gave him away.

Soon afterwards, they set off, having picked up drinking water and packed their small rucksacks. There were a number of trails leading away from the lodge; they could have spent the entire holiday exploring just this section of the rainforest. They set off at a moderate pace, leech socks and all. The vast array of colours still staggered Amy and George, as did the variety of shades of green. Izzy had chosen this trail on purpose because she knew lots of striking exotic blooms were blossoming at this time of year.

Further along the trail Izzy pointed to an explosion of colour, 'Collectors travel from all over the world to trek around Borneo looking for the most exotic flower of them all, the orchid. There are around 18,000 species of orchid and many of them can be found in rainforests.'

'They are quite pretty,' said George, who was not much of a flower lover but even he had to admit how eye-catching they looked.

'They're spectacular,' declared Amy. 'I wish my Mum could see this!'

'There is a down side to them being so alluring. The orchids are often too tempting for the collectors to resist and they pick too many. Sadly this can lead to the orchids becoming very rare or extinct. Just as animals become extinct from too much hunting, so flowers can disappear forever if we don't take care of their environment,' said Izzy.

Amy asked if she could take a few minutes out to sketch the necklace orchid and the stunning yellow slipper orchid that were nearby. She thought her sketches would not do the flowers justice so she asked George to take some photographs.

'This is a good place to stop. When we get further down the trail, it gets much darker and damper. A rainforest has different layers and the heads of the trees form the canopy. These orchids can only grow on the forest floor here because they get some sunlight. I'll show you the opposite of these flowers later,' said Izzy. She was thankful the children were inquisitive because it made guiding them much easier. It also meant that she was not the only one talking all day, as so often happens if escorting big groups of tourists around.

While Amy and George were taking photographs and sketching she began telling them about her favourite orchid. 'I travelled to the Philippines, only a short flight away, to visit my friend. She knew I loved flora so we went exploring. We came across a rare lilac orchid that smelt of rhubarb, looked perfect, fragile yet strong enough to survive high up on a hillside'. Izzy only knew the Latin name of the orchid and it was - '*Dendrobium Superbum*'.

Amy and George turned their faces slightly away from her and had to bite their lips not to laugh out loud. After such a poetic description the orchid had the name 'superbum'. Izzy would not have understood their toilet humour, so they carried on with what they were doing, but they had a laugh about it later on in the day.

They continued down the trail and George saw some tasty looking berries hanging down from a nearby branch. Just as he was going to pick one, Izzy grabbed his wrist and stopped him, 'Sorry George but I don't think that's a good idea. Some berries are okay to eat and others can cause you great discomfort. This is one subject I'm not the expert on. Terangu, the tribesmen, will answer all your questions on the good and bad berries. Having lived his life in the rainforest, he's an expert. That reminds me, I'll have to give you a few 'dos' and 'don'ts' of living in a longhouse. I know you're not going there for a few days but it's good to give the rules a few days to sink in.'

'Don't worry, we'll try not to embarrass you,' joshed George.

'They're a lovely family but much more traditional than most. They've no TV or radio like most families who live in longhouses. It will help you to know the simple customs beforehand.'

They pressed on further into the rainforest and it became darker and darker. The thickening canopy above caused increased shade below. Amy noticed her clothes sticking to her more and more, as if she had been walking in the rain. Izzy explained that the lack of sunlight, large trees, thicker canopy and lack of wind added to the humidity. The increased water vapour in the air was making their clothes wet, sticky and uncomfortable. Amy and George noticed that there were less brightly coloured flowers around. George walked on further and pointed to some odd looking vegetation.

'Mushroom omelette anyone? I certainly won't be trying them!'

'Good spot George. Look at the canopy above; a large branch has broken off and the fungi are growing in the only patch getting any sunlight. They would be brown or a blackish grey if they had no sunlight, certainly not red. All fungi grow quickly down here on the damp, mossy, forest floor. They use the nutrients or minerals from the dead matter all around them. Rotting leaves and decaying animals never go to waste in the rainforest. Certain mushrooms are edible, although it can be very dangerous to eat the wrong ones. Some are poisonous and others are hallucinogenic, which means they cause the mind to play tricks and see things that are not there. There are other types of fungi all around us, so go and have a scout around.'

'It's easy to see why you love your job so much Izzy. You get to see such a cool variety of animals, plants, fruits, insects, reptiles and even uninviting fungi. It changes every second of every day and we both love it out here!' commented Amy. George nodded and gave them the thumbs up to show he was in complete agreement.

Just as Izzy was about to suggest they head back, something on the forest floor caught her eye. The children took a step back to find out what she was looking at. There must have been hundreds, if not thousands of orange and rusty red coloured ants all over the floor. These ants were much bigger than any Amy and George had seen back home.

'These are fire ants and there must be a colony around here or an awful lot of food to draw so many out at one time,' said Izzy.

They spread out and looked around the surrounding area. After a few minutes Izzy called them over, 'Look at these giants.' On the blade of her penknife were two ants ready for inspection. 'Look how large the mandibles are, compared to the rest of the body.' From the baffled look she received from the pair she continued explaining, 'Mandibles are a part of the jaw and are used for biting and gripping things. These soldier ants have to protect the thousands of worker ants from other ant colonies. The small but busy worker ants serve an important role because they ferry the food back to the nest where the queen is. These soldiers cannot survive without them.'

'Why do the super strong soldier ants need any help from the smaller worker ants,' enquired George.

'Every single ant in a colony has a particular job to do. The soldier ants have big problems feeding themselves. They are built for fighting and protecting the colony; that is why they have these huge mandibles. The worker ants have to help feed the soldiers like babies and the queen has to lay eggs so the colony can expand,' revealed Izzy.

'Ants will never look the same again after this trip,' said George.

'Once a colony of ants has stripped an area of rainforest, they literally pick everything up and move their home to a different place. There's an ant in the jungles of Africa called the 'driver ant' that even elephants avoid. Completely blind, but terrifying because they rip prey apart with their large mandibles, they kill snakes, lizards and mammals just with their sheer weight of numbers. Some colonies may have as many as 22 million in them!' said Izzy.

An unfamiliar but foul smell made George's nose twitch. He took another long sniff, 'Can you two not smell that?'

Amy moved closer and sniffed the air. 'Perhaps it's another Rafflesia plant underneath those overhanging leaves?' She lifted the leaves to reveal a gruesome sight. There were thousands of fire ants teaming over a rotting piece of meat.

'Yuk! That's gross. What is it?' said Amy, recoiling in disgust.

Using a stick to pick up the bloody object, Izzy turned and laid it down on the small clearing. She shook it and brushed off most of the ants to get a closer look. After some hesitancy Izzy said, 'This is a piece of carrion or should I say, rotting pig flesh! Something has killed a pig and left part of it here!'

'Why would an animal kill its prey, eat some and then leave the rest for the ants?'

'I'm not sure Amy; let's have a quick look and then head back to the lodge,' replied Izzy.

They split up and began to have a nose around the surrounding area. Not long after that Amy came across a second piece of stinking, rotting meat that instantly made her feel queasy. Using a long stick, Amy moved the rotting pig steak next to the other one on the clearing. Before Amy could call out to Izzy about her find, she heard a spine-chilling scream. Knowing it was George made her feel sick to the pit of her stomach. Izzy was nowhere to be seen. Amy could hear George screaming but could not work out where he was. His screams were getting closer each second. Amy was paralysed with fear; even if she could have moved, she had no idea in which direction to run.

George was sprinting at full pelt. He was petrified because he knew that one slip and he could be mincemeat.

The closer he got, the clearer his voice sounded to Amy. She could now clearly hear the urgency and terror as he yelled, 'Climb! Climb! Climb!'

Amy dropped her stick and began to climb the closest tree. The bark was damp due to the humidity and it crumbled in her hands like papier-mâché. She frantically tried to clamber up the tree to safety but only got a metre off the ground before falling backwards onto the clearing. An ear splitting grunting was closing in at high-speed and she was getting nowhere fast. Amy tried desperately to distance herself from the furious rustling and crashing but lost her footing. Her nerves were shot to pieces with worry for herself and George. Something was drawing ever closer to her and she was on her backside, powerless.

Suddenly, George burst through the nearby undergrowth and in one movement pulled Amy up by her collar. He gave her a boost up onto the first branch of the tree and using his remaining strength, he shinned up the tree as if his life depended upon it.

Amy turned and screamed out to Izzy, whom she still could not see, 'Climb Izzy, Climb NOW!' Amy put a soothing hand on George's shoulder to try and calm him. She had never seen George like this. He was next to her on the branch shaking profusely and barely able to catch his breath. A look of sheer panic was etched across his sweat stained face.

Izzy was now no further than ten metres away from them. She heard Amy scream and leapt for the closest branch. They were all off the forest floor just in the nick of time.

Seconds later, a fast-moving, colossal, grunting, black mass of spiky hair appeared from the undergrowth. Two more great beasts careered from the same direction. They trampled the vegetation in their path so that it was as flat as Holland. Amy and George were in the tree scared out of their wits watching these three behemoths. They had no idea what was going to happen next but were thankful they were up a tree and not on the clearing below. These powerful beasts looked like crazed prehistoric wart hogs or giant pigs mutated by a nuclear explosion. Their tusks stuck far out from their lower jaws. The beasts were causing mayhem, their stomping felt as if they were trying to shake the children out of their hiding place.

The children silently wished that the branch would not give way under their combined weight. The mixture of squeals and grunts made them think of horror movies their parents would never let them watch, except children always see them at sleepovers or at Halloween. The two beasts making the most noise were now circling each other menacingly. The third was hovering at the clearings edge like the referee in a boxing match as the two sized each other up. Something had to give.

Izzy shouted from the tree she was perched in, 'Stay there and don't move until I tell you!' They could not hear a word Izzy said over the furore below but they had absolutely no intention of getting down from where they were.

The larger beast exploded into life, he slashed ferociously at his opponent with his razor sharp tusks. This first attack wounded the other badly; the children saw blood spurt out of a deep gash on its side. The injured animal let out a deafening squeal, only to be slashed and gashed, again and again. The well-built animal was using the full force of its massive frame to slice into the smaller one's side with its deadly tusks. Amy and George had to look away as blood and guts poured out of his belly. Injured beyond recovery, the smaller one ran off squealing in mortal pain. This wounded animal would become food for a stronger predator later that day.

Amy and George looked down onto the clearing, wondering if fight two was on the cards. However, the larger beast chose the king size rotting steak and began to tuck in. This was the sign for the other to start carefully gnawing away at the second smaller piece of meat whilst still keeping an eye on the victor. Having gnawed at his ant covered victory meal for a while, the largest one picked up what was left of his steak with his hefty jaws and wandered off in the direction of the loser. Amy and George let out a sigh of relief because he was the angriest, most ill tempered animal they had ever come across in their short lives. They were glad to see his jumbo tail-end as he retreated into the rainforest. The remaining beast took his time to finish the carrion steak and let out a grunt of satisfaction once it was finished. Luckily, he also headed off in the opposite direction from the trail leading to the lodge.

'Are you okay?' shouted Izzy, who had been trembling with concern.

'Fine!' shouted Amy shakily.

'Cooking on gas!' declared George, trying to act tough as if this were an everyday event.

The children were stunned at what they had seen, only a few metres away from where they were precariously perched.

'You've just witnessed a rare event, a fight between full-grown male wild boars. They're a distant relation of the pigs you have in England,' noted Izzy.

'By the look of those brutes, I'd say an extremely distant relation to the small, friendly pigs we're used to,' remarked Amy.

'Maybe a third cousin, twice removed on the great aunt's side that married into the family,' added George, trying to lighten the mood. Amy gave a pig-like snort as she laughed, causing a joint fit of the giggles.

CHAPTER EIGHT

What felt like an eternity had passed since the last wild boar had taken off, although it was only half an hour. The calming songs of the crickets and cicadas had replaced the noise of the brawling boars and their foul-tempered grunting. Izzy got down from the tree and had a scout around. She turned back when she heard the children yelping, 'Ouch, ow, blast!'

'Izzy, we've got to get down. These pesky fire ants are biting us now they've had their lunch stolen,' shrieked George with a grimace as he was bitten again.

'Okay, but we must head straight back to the lodge!' Izzy helped them down and they walked briskly back along the trail.

'Those animals eat roots, fruit, fungi and occasionally small mammals and reptiles. They must have got a whiff of the carrion when we moved it out into the open. They are very fast and have good noses so they could have smelt the carrion from some distance away,' observed Izzy, mainly to herself.

'I for one am glad they didn't *carrion* for too long,' jested George.

Amy let out a sigh at George's continued poor attempts at animal humour. The children chatted away about this cannibal member of the pig family, eating those rotting pig steaks. They hurried along after Izzy who was in a world of her own.

Before they reached the lodge Amy slowed up and whispered, 'Thanks George. Thanks for helping me out back there. The tree was mega slippery and I lost my footing the second time. I couldn't have got up there without you.'

'It's no problem, I just thought your tree looked big enough for both of us and I didn't want you to *hog* the best spot.' George chortled at his own joke and Amy gave him a cheesy smile in return. 'I'm glad I was around to save your *bacon*. Only kidding, you were kind enough to invite me on this holiday in the first place. The least I can do is to give you a bunk up a tree, away from a few little piggies!'

'You're a joker, George Cooke but I'm glad we're friends.'

They carried on walking and soon caught up with Izzy but then Amy noticed George blushing. He was not used to compliments except from his Mum, Helen. George felt chuffed inside; he had done exactly what his father asked. He had helped his friend and stayed by her side even though they were both scared. Although, being a lad, he would never admit to being terrified! Apart from the fear, he was overjoyed to have seen a battle between two big, brutal, bloodthirsty boars. It was the most exciting day of his whole life.

Amy noticed a spectacular bird pecking away at the ground near the lodge. It had an apricot coloured beak, red head, white and yellow breast and turquoise feathers. 'What a stunning bird to greet us home,' she said.

'It's a Jambu fruit dove and the first I've seen in months. A pleasant surprise,' said Izzy. Another photograph for the records, they certainly had a few more animals, birds and insects to add to a growing holiday list.

'Have a rest for half an hour and then get showered and changed, we can relax and have some lunch. Okay with you two?' asked Izzy. Both children nodded.

When they met for a late lunch, Izzy had something she wanted to get off her chest.

'Amy, George. I'm sorry to have put you in danger. I've never seen wild boars act like that, especially so near to here. They go a little crazy in the mating season but that's months away. Normally they are nocturnal creatures and try to avoid humans!'

The children saw how upset she was at the day's events. George let Amy speak first because he knew she was much more likely to choose the right words. The kind approach was called for and this was not the time for his larking around.

'Izzy, we don't blame you in the slightest. We're back safe and sound. No harm has been done and we're having a brilliant time!'

'I'm having plenty of fun but I could do with something to stop the ant bites from itching,' added George, scratching his bites.

Izzy was relieved that they did not want her to drive them straight to the airport, so they could board the first aeroplane bound for home. She left the table and went to her medical cupboard. She pulled out a tiny pot, 'Put this on your bites, it will feel hot at first and may sting but it does help.' Izzy handed the pot of *tiger balm* to Amy saying it could also help with any sore, aching muscles. They both applied the balm which began to work instantly. They could now concentrate solely on tucking into a hearty lunch and not scratching their painful bites.

Izzy had not told the children all of her concerns regarding the morning's event. She had been thinking about a change of plans, in light of them having almost been crushed to death by wild boars; weighing 200 kilograms and standing nearly one metre in height. 'I've been giving our schedule some thought. I think we should go and stay at Terangu's longhouse earlier than expected. I know you're keen to learn as much as possible and Terangu knows so much about the local plants and wildlife. The area he lives in is incredible. I'm sure he'll have his dartboards out ready for a blowpipe contest,' added Izzy. She did not add that she thought they would be much safer there.

'You don't mean we have to go right away, not this afternoon Izzy?' stammered George.

This was exactly what Izzy meant, as she was deeply concerned by what had happened.

Before she could answer, Amy made a suggestion, 'If it's okay, could we leave first thing tomorrow morning? This would give us the chance to go out in the boat and have a quick look for the long-nosed monkeys. We'd have time to learn the rules of living in the longhouse over dinner and still have loads of time to pack before bed. We could get cracking early tomorrow morning, refreshed and ready to boogie!' Secretly, Amy was not keen on going out in the boat after the morning's unpleasant incident. However, she felt she owed it to George to at least make the suggestion. He had been so looking forward to learning how to pilot the boat.

Izzy did not want to argue the point because the children had been great about their brush with danger that morning. She did not want to alarm them further by insisting on leaving the lodge immediately. Izzy thought for a minute. If they were out in the boat this afternoon what more trouble could they get into? She nodded in agreement to what appeared to be a sensible plan. George's spirits visibly lifted as he was much happier with this idea.

'Will Terangu mind us going earlier than planned and possibly staying longer, Izzy?' enquired George.

'It'll be fine, I told him to expect us sometime over the period you were here. Maybe we could stop upriver at the market early tomorrow so you could buy a small gift. It's one of the traditional customs when guests stay at a longhouse. Even taking vegetables or some meat for a stew would be fine,' said Izzy.

'Our parents gave us a little spending money and we both have pocket money saved up, so that's no problem. When you're staying over at a friend's house in England, you usually take chocolates or something similar,' replied Amy.

'Amy and I haven't spent a ringitt yet; but then we haven't seen many shops this holiday apart from a few at the airport,' remarked George. They were glad to have the plan settled and could now enjoy lunch, all the excitement had given them monstrous appetites.

When they got into the boat that afternoon they fastened their lifejackets, just in case. Better to be safe than sorry after the morning they had had. Izzy untied the boat and took them out away from the riverbank. Izzy asked George to check for any other boats on this stretch of the river. 'Well George, now's your chance!' said Izzy.

George babbled on for a minute about his Dad wanting him to learn something new every day but he was obviously trying to cover up his nerves. Izzy switched the boat off so he could start from the beginning.

'Attach this cord to the belt of your lifejacket, this leads to an emergency stop switch. If you fell overboard, it would yank this cord out and stop the engine. You can avoid this by staying seated when in control of the boat. Flick this small tap underneath the engine and pull the starter cord' - this was just like the cord from his parents' old lawnmower. 'This will start the propeller turning slowly and if you twist the throttle here, the boat goes faster. The throttle is like the one on a motorbike. The further you twist it round, the quicker the propeller goes and the quicker the boat goes. If you think we're going too fast or the water is getting choppy then ease the throttle back. I won't explain going in reverse just yet,' said Izzy.

'Thank goodness for that! You just concentrate on us going forward, Captain George,' said Amy light-heartedly.

Izzy continued, 'To steer, turn the throttle grip left if you want to go left and right if you want to go right. Steering a small propeller isn't like steering a large boat with a rudder. In a big boat or yacht you go in the opposite way, left is right and vice-versa.'

George was finally settled at the helm, strapped in and raring to go. He flicked the tap, pulled the cord and turned the throttle whilst pointing the boat up the river. He was as quiet as Amy had ever seen; concentrating hard on what he was doing. Izzy got him to practise steering right then left, speeding up and slowing down to a crawl. George was a natural and in half an hour he had everything under control. At this point, a happier twelve-year-old was not to be found anywhere on the planet. Once Izzy was satisfied that Captain George was confident at the helm, she moved forward to join Amy.

'Hi Izzy, George mentioned to me that you'd lost your penknife when those wild boars charged. I'd like you to have mine because my Mum doesn't know I've got one and I haven't even used it that much. George has always got his if I need to borrow it.'

'That's thoughtful of you but I couldn't accept something so expensive from you.' replied Izzy.

'Well, at least borrow it while we're here, you never know when you'll need one.'

'Okay Amy, that's kind of you. Thanks for the loan.'

They both had their binoculars out, scouring the banks for the missing long-nosed monkeys. They saw the odd macaque monkey, some hornbills and a selection of raptors out hunting. Now and then, Amy or Izzy pointed to an area of the riverbank that needed closer inspection and 'Cappy' as Amy was now calling George would duly oblige. After a few hours of searching, the light began to fade, so a disappointed Izzy, asked George to head back towards the lodge.

They were a short distance from the lodge when George thought he spied something perched on a tree stump. 'Ladies, can you use your binoculars to check over there please! I'll aim the boat in that direction?'

Amy was first to focus her binoculars where he had pointed. She immediately let out a squeal of delight, 'Bravo Cappy, a one hundred percent confirmed sighting of a long-nosed monkey. What else has a very long nose, potbelly and red, orange fur?'

George was beaming and Amy was over the moon but Izzy still looked dejected.

'What's wrong Izzy, surely this is a good sign?' queried a puzzled Amy.

'I'm not so sure! I've never seen one this close to the lodge before. Also, he's on his own! Where is the rest of the troop? There's not a single female on that whole section of riverbank. A male is naturally attractive to females with that big nose of his. The females can't help themselves and always end up hanging around the male of the species. He should have a harem with him!'

This rather took the shine off an unforgettable moment for the children. To see an animal in the wild for the first time is a breathtaking experience, particularly when it is one as rare as the male proboscis monkey. Izzy's comments had worried the intrepid explorers even more. Amy and George had thought the mystery was closer to being solved, not further away. They edged closer in the boat to get photographic evidence to prove they had seen at least one proboscis monkey this holiday. The solitary monkey was inactive, not even taking part in his favourite pastime; eating shoots and leaves. They thought he actually looked a little lonely.

After observing the monkey for about half an hour, something startled him and he took off for cover in the thick foliage. The children sat for a while in silence; listening, thinking and trying to take it all in. Eventually Izzy showed George how to use the reverse gear and they headed back to the lodge for dinner. The initial excitement of having seen their first proboscis monkey was outweighed by their anxiety to solve this mystery. They were all worried as to where the others could be; how could so many monkeys be missing?

While Amy and George got ready for dinner, George tried to lighten the mood somewhat,

'For a rest day, we've seen some action. A short lie-in followed by a relaxing walk, topped off by getting attacked by food-crazy boars, bitten by fire ants and then our first sighting of the bizarre long-nosed monkey. No one will believe us back home!'

'It's been the most wonderful but weirdest day of my life. I'm glad we've shared it but …. I'm sure there's more to those rotting pig steaks than Izzy let on. I didn't want to ask her too many questions because she was so upset about what had happened,' observed Amy.

'Okay Sherlock, you have a point! Add that together with how sad Izzy was when we saw just one monkey in the wrong part of town. Let's keep it to ourselves because it's been a very long day for her. She must be a nervous wreck after we came so close to being squished by those bloodthirsty boars. Imagine her having to write, 'Dear Mr and Mrs Applegate, we are sorry to inform you that a giant pig has squashed your daughter!"

'You're awful! That's a beastly thought but possibly the reason why we're on our way to Terangu's earlier than planned. Let's make our notes on the longhouse rules over dinner, and not ask too many questions. After that we'll get back here, pack and then go straight to bed? Let's worry about what tomorrow brings, tomorrow.'

'No problem, I'm knackered already,' replied George with a big yawn.

Most of the rules Izzy told them were pretty basic and things that were 'taboo' in their own or friends' houses. Izzy thought it best to prepare them for living with a family, cut off from most of modern society. Remove your shoes on entry to the house; do not spit on the floor or blow your nose at the table during dinner and do not point your feet at anyone sitting on the floor mats near you. Always try a small amount of the food, whatever it may be and when accepting food from someone, take it from him or her with both hands. They made the list but neither Amy nor George was worried because they were straightforward enough.

'What kind of gift can we buy for Terangu's family when we go to the market tomorrow?' asked Amy.

'Don't worry; I'm sure that something will catch your eye. You never know what is going to be on sale at the market until you get there,' answered Izzy.

They enjoyed a relaxed dinner together after what had been a hectic day. Before Amy and George could excuse themselves from the table, Izzy thanked them again for being so understanding about the morning's near disaster. The children assured her that it was a freak occurrence and not her fault in the slightest. They said their 'goodnights' before Amy and George went to their room to pack their rucksacks. When they got into their beds they ached from head to toe. They chatted briefly about the peculiar primate puzzle before drifting off to the comforting zither of the cicadas.

CHAPTER NINE

As the new day began to break, Izzy came and rapped lightly on the door to see if they were stirring. The children were already awake and sitting on their beds writing their travel journals. They had awoken as soon as the sun lifted its luminous head. Both had slept soundly with no dark dreams of screeching boars or flying cockroaches.

'I'll be serving breakfast in twenty minutes if that's okay?' said Izzy.

'That'll be fine as long as I get to wash before Goldilocks here. I'm always finished in a few minutes,' jibed George.

'That's true but only because you don't wash properly, Cappy! You're famous for the splash and dash technique,' retorted Amy. George had no comeback, so just nodded his head and laughed.

'I'll leave you two comedians to get ready. See you in twenty minutes,' said Izzy.

They enjoyed a large breakfast of local fruit followed by an omelette and rice, washed down with mango juice. Feeling replete, Amy and George loaded their bags onto the boat and headed up river not knowing what lay ahead. Izzy only let George pilot the boat for the first section because they would definitely come across traffic on the river today, being market day. When Izzy took over, George happily kicked back and enjoyed the scenery. The wildlife was out in force again on this fine morning; a wrinkled bill hornbill, a few herons and a family of macaques. As they passed other boats and canoes, the locals smiled at them and waved enthusiastically. Amy noticed that the traffic was heading for a clearing on the riverbank ahead. There were dugout wooden canoes, boats similar in size to theirs and a homemade raft that looked very rickety.

A young boy waved to Izzy and shouted a greeting, she threw him the rope and he tied her boat up. 'Leave your bags on the boat but don't forget your wallets. It's okay to haggle a little but please do it with a smile and remember how much more your money is worth!' noted Izzy.

They would not have noticed the clearing if it had not been for the boat traffic and a couple of makeshift wooden stalls. A few locals had their goods laid out on foldaway tables. Amy's godfather Simon and her uncle Olly regularly took them both to boot fairs. Apart from being on a much smaller scale, that is what it reminded her of. Everyone had a few knick-knacks to sell, as well as their main products. A woman, who looked in her eighties, kept swiping at flies constantly landing on the fish she had for sale. She also had old earthenware pots stashed haphazardly under her table. A young man, who was sitting by a stack of trays filled with chicken eggs, ran a sideline selling local cigarettes and tobacco.

Their first attempt at buying something came when they saw a woman selling everything from soft-boiled eggs to sticky rice wrapped in a banana leaf and something resembling uncooked spring rolls. This woman had her goods in plastic trays that looked cleaner than some other stalls. Amy and George had been worried about buying food from a hawker stall, in case they got a bad stomach.

Amy asked the woman how much, 'Berapa?' Izzy whispered the name of what she was pointing at, 'Berapa roti kaya?' continued a nervous Amy. She felt the butterflies in her tummy but should not have worried. The locals appreciated any tourists; especially children who tried to speak their language. The woman raised one finger and smiled a toothy grin at Amy. She paid one ringitt and was pleasantly surprised at how good the delicacy tasted. She had bought a fried piece of bread with coconut egg jam on top. She let out a satisfied 'Mmhh!' and bought another two, one for Izzy and George. After reminding George that one pound was worth about six ringitt, he thought that this could well be the best sixteen pence snack ever made.

George found out the name of the cake he wanted and then asked the old woman, 'Berapa shou tao?' She again held up one finger and smiled. George got a surprise; his was filled with a strong-tasting spicy red-bean paste. He managed to eat it and thank her but it was too fiery for him. Amy and Izzy politely refused when he offered to buy another two cakes for them.

'Do many of the locals here speak English, Izzy?' asked George.

Izzy told them that some can speak English fluently and others spoke Pidgin English, a very basic form of

English. Most knew at least the numbers in English so that they could haggle if a larger tourist boat came down this stretch of the Kinabatangan River.

They came to a man who had a number of live animals for sale. 'George, why don't we club together and get them a chicken? That would be useful,' suggested Amy.

'We could do, but why don't we ask how much that small blotchy piglet is?'

'Isn't he adorable? I don't like the thought of him ending up on the dinner table George.'

The stall owner smiled a gap-toothed smile and said in pidgin English, 'Long time no see, gut pipel.'

'Good morning,' replied Amy, 'How much is that pig please?'

'Em is baby pik, yutupela. No sah, yu want diss gut pik. Look-see, look-see,' the stall owner exclaimed cheerfully. He pointed to a much fatter, much noisier but plainer looking pig. The children had their hearts set on the runt of the litter, so politely declined his offer. He initially wanted 180 ringitt for the piglet, which the children thought was a large sum of money. Amy did a quick estimation and it worked out to be around thirty pounds.

George scratched his chin and shook his head ever so slightly. He did not realise the haggling process had begun and the price immediately came down to 120 ringitt. Amy and George were jubilant; they sealed the deal by exchanging handshakes and each paying the stall owner 60 ringitt.

The seller scooped the little pig up and handed him to Amy, 'Im get gut haus now! Bye pik, bye gut pipel.'

'He'll be a worthy addition to Terangu's family,' said Izzy with a broad smile.

'How can this happy little pig, be related to those boorish boars?' said Amy.

George and Izzy smiled at the thought of those bloodthirsty boars compared to the contented little pig being held in Amy's arms.

'Considering how expensive wine and chocolates are at home, this was a bargain,' observed George. The children were delighted with their purchase, the first piglet they had ever bought. The piglet did not squeal or struggle and Amy could not help but admire his patchy colours, a pinkish brown with black patches on his side.

The happy shoppers bought local vegetables and got necklaces as presents for their Mums and George's two aunts, Liz and Sophie. Izzy did not have a chance to tell them that Terangu's wife made beautiful necklaces. Izzy and George boarded the boat with the supplies and then Amy offloaded the piglet to George while she got on. As soon as the piglet was in George's hands, it decided to answer the call of nature. The piglet began to tinkle all down his t-shirt. It was not just a little tinkle either; it was as if the piglet had saved up his whole mornings supply. Amy burst into a fit of laughter and almost fell overboard. It went on his hands, shorts, shoes and t-shirt. It took George a while to see the funny side but he could not stay mad at the piglet for very long. It looked so happy, snuffling around inside the boat smelling their feet.

Izzy took them further along the river and pointed towards the bank. Amy and George could not see what was there but Izzy explained that it was one of the many small rivers or tributaries leading off the main river. Many tribal families did not want to live right next to the main river because there was less privacy and more noise from passing boats.

The noise level rose when they began travelling along the tributary. They were close to nature again. The grating of the bamboo as the wind rushed past it, the insect and bird calls coming from all around them. Amy and George felt privileged to be seeing a place few people might ever see. They both had a build up of butterflies in their stomachs. Their nervousness was because of what lay ahead, could a tribal family be so different from their own? Amy and George had got used to life without their computers, televisions, the Internet, traffic jams, supermarkets and games consoles. They were thoroughly enjoying the simple life and their new surroundings. They stopped worrying when they saw some cheery young children shouting and waving from the riverbank, causing quite a stir.

'We're here. Let's tie up the boat and go and find Terangu. I'm sure he'll have heard the children and guessed we've arrived,' said Izzy.

Amy and George caught a glimpse of where they would be sleeping, a massive longhouse on wooden stilts; it was a tall and impressive structure. A weathered older man with a feather in his headgear was making his way towards them. Amy noticed that he had tattoos covering his body. By the time they had their bags on firm ground the children were moving amongst them, trying to get a glimpse of the piglet. They quietened down when Terangu arrived.

'Hello Izzy my friend. Good to see you. These must be your two new friends from a land faraway?' asked Terangu.

'Terangu, this is Amy,' who stepped forward, shook his hand and bowed her head to her elder, 'and this is George. They've been keen students and eager to learn.'

Amy took a few steps back and stooped down to pick up the piglet and presented it to Terangu saying, 'We'd like you to have this as a thank you for letting us stay in your home.'

'We will both try to help wherever possible,' added George.

Terangu was taken aback by their generosity and kind words. He handed the pig to the tallest boy and whispered something to him. All the children scurried after him and began to busy themselves with the chores. Amy hoped he had not told the boy to go and kill the pig!

'My full name is Terangu-melayu Mathahir of the Orang Ulu tribe but as Izzy has already told you, I'm normally called Terangu. That's fine for both of you? Not too difficult to remember I hope!' he joked.

'From now on we'll call you Terangu, Terangu,' declared Amy politely.

'It has a nice ring to it,' added George, who really thought Tel might have been a better choice.

A smile came across Terangu's face and he picked up their bags and led them towards the longhouse to show them their sleeping quarters. The steps leading up to the longhouse veranda were huge logs with V-shapes cut out, to put your feet on. The simplicity of the steps greatly impressed the children. Terangu noticed Amy looking at the steps and assumed she was looking at the patterns carved on either side of the log steps and on the handrails.

'My oldest son, Rigu, is now better than me with his carvings. I carved the designs on the stilt legs but Rigu has done the shutters, the steps, the banisters and even the tools,' said Terangu, proud of his son's work.

In fact, everywhere Amy looked there were beautiful swirling designs. The unique carvings added something special to the longhouse because it instantly felt like a home. Amy marvelled at the size of the veranda; the fireplaces 'inside' the wooden longhouse; the carved wooden shutters that were locked in an upright position above the gaps which were the equivalent of windows. Hanging along the inside walls was a vast collection of extraordinary items: hats, baskets, spears, metallic gongs and even an old-fashioned sword and wooden shield. Eventually they came to the far end of the longhouse that was as long as its name suggested. Terangu showed them where they would be sleeping and asked Izzy to explain about the mosquito nets, while he checked on his family.

'Oh, Izzy, this place is fantastic,' enthused Amy.

There were reed mats with very thin, feather filled mattresses on top. They had one small cushion-like object each to rest their heads on, no sheets, pillowcases or duvets. The mosquito nets were attached to the wall and could be pulled out along the two cords that acted like shower curtain rails, tied to the walls.

'There are only two beds here Izzy, where are you going to sleep?'

'Don't worry! I'm not going to leave you on your first night. I've packed a sleeping mat and sleeping bag, so I can squeeze in between you this evening, if you don't mind?'

They heard a thunderous noise coming from the veranda and then felt the vibrations through the wooden floor. On hearing the gong Izzy told them that lunch was now ready.

'One last thing, as some members of the family don't speak English let them see that you understand their customs, try all the food and don't forget to accept plates with both hands.' said Izzy.

'We won't let you down,' said George convincingly. Izzy knew they would try but it would be tricky with noisy young children around and not being able to understand everything being said.

The longhouse was divided up by a number of wooden partitions that acted as the walls of the different rooms. There were no doors meaning there was little privacy. The wonderful aroma from the food was spreading like wildfire. They could smell the dishes before they feasted their eyes upon them. Izzy was unsure if they would like the food. So far she had cooked them simple dishes, boneless fish in tomato and herb sauce, sweet and sour chicken, omelettes, fresh vegetables and noodle stir-fry but nothing too spicy.

A wobbly wooden table had clearly been added to the usual one, to fit the extra guests. Terangu gestured to Amy, George and Izzy to sit down in the three free seats at the middle of the table. The three ancient grandparents, whose combined age was over 250 years, spoke no English. The one grandparent who had learnt to speak English was unfortunately no longer alive. Terangu and his wife Pantai, whose name means beach, could both speak English very well. Pantai's sister and husband plus their four children - three girls and a boy, spoke little or no English. The remaining two older boys, who were rushing to and fro serving food, were Terangu's children. Terangu had already told them about his eldest, Rigu, who was nearly seventeen. The younger brother called Tema was fourteen. Amy and George were introduced to the whole family and later they jotted down a family tree in their journals to help them remember the names.

Rigu began to pour a peculiar looking liquid into the guests' miniature cups. Terangu addressed the table first in Malay and then English. He welcomed the two guests to his home and hoped they enjoyed the food. Terangu spoke of only two guests because Izzy was considered to be part of the family.

Amy and George both replied, 'Terima kasih banyak – thank you very much.'

Following the grandparents' lead, they drank the thimbleful of liquid down in one quick gulp. Amy and George tried hard not to cough or splutter after downing the contents of the cup. Anyone who has ever seen their parents' faces when they drink a large shot of neat whisky will understand the face that Amy and George made. The mystery drink had a foul taste, which turned into an uncomfortable burning sensation the whole way down their throats, only to be followed by an unusual warming sensation from the bottom of their stomachs outwards. When they began to fan their breath as if they had just eaten a hot chilli, the grandparents let out a roar of approval. They motioned for Tema to pour some more drinks and between their hysterics they downed another and raised their empty cups to Amy and George saying, 'Baik tuak!'

Not wanting to spoil the grandparents' fun, George lifted his cup. At this point Amy looked at him in astonishment because she knew she would have to follow suit.

'Baik tuak,' said George after he sank his second drink with a grimace and then a smile, raising his empty cup to the delight of the grandparents.

Amy was aghast at having to drink another one but did so out of politeness. She thought it was a horrible mixture of cough medicine and mouthwash. Still, she downed it and raised her cup saying, 'Baik tuak!' as an involuntary shudder went right through her.

Izzy explained that 'baik' meant 'good' and 'tuak' meant 'rice wine,' which was the local alcoholic tipple. 'I do hope I'm not going to get into trouble with your parents? Letting minors drink alcohol,' said Izzy.

'We're only honouring our hosts' parents, so I'm sure it's okay,' replied Amy.

George nodded but kept quiet. He was grinning like a Cheshire cat and already had an unhealthy alcoholic glow to his face. He knew only too well that this was Amy's way of saying, 'I won't mention this again if you don't'. Both would pay in the morning for having these drinks with their hosts, a stomachache was guaranteed.

They tucked into the feast set out before them. The first mouth-watering dish was chicken and herbs cooked inside bamboo. The next dish was 'kway-teow' and bamboo shoots, a mixture of rice flour noodles and spear shaped shoots from the bamboo plant. After watching the grandparents eat the sticky rice with their hands, they thought it rude not to do the same. Deep-fried Malaysian spring rolls, filled with yam beans and locally grown peppers followed. Bang-kuang and kway-teow, sounded much more exotic than bangers and mash or beans on toast.

Amy and George were having an eating extravaganza, especially as the horrible liquor had given them a vigorous appetite. Terangu's nephews and nieces were rarely at the table, coming and going as they pleased, picking at a little food here and there.

The grandparents were enjoying the feast most of all. They ate ravenously and had as much of an appetite for the rice wine as anything else. They were getting merrier and merrier as the lunch went on. Questions were being asked from all sides of the table, the answers and questions were being translated back and forth in both languages.

Terangu's boys began to clear the empty plates and bowls. Terangu whispered something to Rigu and he disappeared outside. They had been cooking on both the veranda and inside the longhouse on the fire. They had an area that was boxed in with stones and filled with sand, an indoor cooking sandpit. There was a small flue leading up to a wooden shutter acting like a chimney. This meant they could safely burn wood inside and the smoke would rise up and out of the open shutter. There was another opening higher up which could be closed in case of rain. It was the most ingenious kitchen you could ever imagine.

Rigu returned to the table and placed a bowl in front of Amy and George, 'As our guests, this local delicacy is served to you first. I'm not sure if the word is correct, 'dessert' perhaps.'

Amy and George did not know what to make of it. Terangu saw them examining it closely and gave them some advice, 'They taste better if you remove the wings and legs because they get stuck between your teeth.'

The assortment of insects had been cooked to a crisp, so they looked like chips that had been left in the oven too long. Some bits looked like the pork crackling you get with a roast dinner. Not wanting to offend their hosts, they picked up a fried cricket; plucking its wings and legs off and taking a bite. It tasted salty but was not as bad as they had expected.

'Very tasty, thank you,' murmured Amy. If she closed her eyes, it could easily have been crisps that she was crunching.

After the biscuit brown crickets, came large grasshoppers and then some succulent water bugs. The water bugs were the only problem for Amy because she found them too squishy on the inside. Amy and George thought their rainforest trial was finished when yet another dessert was brought out.

George almost threw up, 'Awesome, what a treat. My friends will be so jealous when they find out I've eaten these!' His smile and sarcasm hid the fact that his nightmares had come to haunt him at lunchtime.

'You can't eat all cockroaches but these ones are good. They eat lots of sugary food so have a sweet flavour,' said a beaming Terangu.

Amy pulled off the wings and legs before thanking her host and taking a bite. She kept telling herself it was a homemade biscuit, crunchy on the outside and sweet in the middle. She bravely chewed it and swallowed it but she would never forget that awful lingering taste in her mouth.

George was cautiously examining the dish to see which of the remaining ones was the smallest. He could not get the sea of cockroaches out of his head, also knowing that those cockroaches fed on bat and bird poo. Amy kicked him under the table to hurry him along. He selected one, plucking the legs and wings before scoffing it whole. He crunched it twice in his mouth before swallowing it down.

The grandparents laughed their heads off before Pantai's mother got Rigu to pass her the remaining two. She crunched, sucked and chewed them with gusto as if they were the finest caviar.

'They give you more energy than pork and chicken, as well as being rich in vitamins and minerals,' said Izzy. She explained that the insects they had eaten contained more protein than many foods they ate at home.

'That's all very well but no-one else seems to be tucking in to the bug banquet, except for Grandma over there,' replied George briskly, with a pesky piece of cockroach stuck between his teeth.

Terangu finally spoke up, 'Maybe too much variety on your first day here. I enjoy the crickets, the water bugs are too plain, the grasshoppers give me gas and I can't stomach the cockroaches anymore!'

He retold it in Malay for the benefit of the rest of the family and the longhouse shook with laughter. Amy and George realised this must be part of the family initiation, so took it with a smile.

Once the meal had finished the grandparents went onto the veranda to smoke some stinky homemade cigars that looked like ice-cream cones. The four nephews and nieces slunk off with Tema, leaving Amy and George to help Rigu tidy up. It did not take long to clear up, as there was little waste and what was left was given to the piglet. They knew to make themselves scarce when Izzy began talking to Terangu in Malay.

CHAPTER TEN

Rigu suggested that they take this chance to go and explore outside. Both the children were glad of the chance to stretch their legs after eating so well. They hit it off with Rigu instantly and had a number of questions for him.

'What tribe does your father belong to?' asked George, having not listened carefully when Terangu told them his full name.

'He's always cloudy about this because our family moved upriver away from our roots. My grandparents were the first to settle in this spot, so I suppose we are classed as part of the 'Orang Ulu' tribe or 'up-river dwellers'. The Kinabatangan River is so long, that Orang Ulu could describe people who live hundreds of kilometres apart. Many tribes in Borneo are territorial and have lived in the same area for hundreds of years. There's even a tribe who prefer to roam freely in the rainforest. They only ever settle for a short period before moving on again.'

'What do they do for a food and shelter?' queried Amy

'They find a place with good hunting and then build a shelter. Not like here, just a small hut. It only has to last for a short time, so they try to build near the Sago trees.'

'What food does the Sago produce that's so important?' asked George, still confused.

'At home you eat potatoes and bread. These foods contain sugar and starch, which give you energy. In the rainforest, the Penan tribe rely on the pith of sago tree. They grind up the pith, mash it and the tribeswomen stamp the starch out of the pith over a trough. It's mixed with water, dried and pounded again. They make it into biscuits and other food. To survive they need edible plants, drinking water, fish plus sago biscuits. Sometimes they hunt a few pigs. So the sago palm is a big part of their diet,' explained Rigu.

'How come you know so much about them and who taught you English?' asked George, impressed by Rigu's knowledge and fluency.

'Through Izzy and Terangu; Izzy has been a family friend for many years. She helped me and my brother whenever she could, with lessons and books. As I got better at carving and started to sell and swap them, I often got people to throw in old books as part of the deal. As well as money for carvings, I often get chickens, vegetables, paper, pens,' replied Rigu.

Izzy had helped teach Rigu, so that one day he could help the family as much with his education as his other skills.

'They must be special carvings to get all that for them,' added Amy.

Embarrassed, he quickly changed the subject and showed them the 'Perahu' dugout canoe. He explained that you could use a pole to push yourself along or paddles.

'Don't you have a propeller engine like Izzy?' asked George.

'I've a dirty old one but it rarely works and is not safe to use with this. My friend sometimes loans me his boat if I've got too many carvings for this one. I've used Izzy's before, when she was here helping Terangu.'

George stepped into the canoe and realised that it was much less sturdy than Izzy's boat. They left the canoes and wandered off down one of the trails. They chatted away with Rigu as he pointed out many types of butterflies, birds and flowers. He was such good company that they felt totally at ease with him. Being sixteen, he was an adult and in England he could have left home and got married. Amy and George felt as if they had an older brother around. They both had younger siblings, so this made a pleasant change.

'Here's one of my wooden carvings but *don't* touch it. It's left as a warning!' said Rigu, alerting them to some imminent danger.

'It's beautifully crafted,' enthused Amy.

'What's it warning us about?' asked George, who thought the figure looked marvellous but not at all threatening.

Rigu motioned for them to take a few steps back; he then bounded a full stride ahead. Turning to face them he picked up a large stick and swung it forward, as if he was playing a wild cricket stroke. A bamboo spear came out of nowhere and shot across the trail, embedding itself into a tree trunk on the opposite side. The children were, quite literally, speechless; the carving marked a secret but deadly trap.

'This is a 'peti' trap! Terangu set it up because he's sure there's a plump wild pig nearby. He wanted to catch it to celebrate your arrival but had no luck. He found tracks close by, so it's only a matter of time,' said Rigu.

Amy was horrified that such a treacherous trap was on a trail that one of the young children might walk on. Before she could voice her concerns, Rigu continued.

'These carvings or 'tuntuns' are placed next to the traps to warn people. Few people ever walk along here except my family. Terangu has shown the young ones, many times, how dangerous these traps can be. When you grow up in Borneo, you learn many difficult lessons. Children raised here must learn to hunt but must also learn to respect their environment. I know about the wandering Penan tribe because I've made tuntuns for them. They believe the tuntuns actually attract the pig to the trap. They showed us how to set up the trap properly; the pig trips on the line set across the path. When the vine, cord or thin rope is stretched by the pig's leg, it springs the trap firing the bamboo spear.'

George was like a boy in a sweet shop and could not wait for Rigu to show him how to reset the trap.

'We could've used one of these,' he joked.

Amy explained about the wild boar attack, the rotting pig steaks and watching the boars battle from up a tree.

It was Rigu's turn to be lost for words, 'You were very lucky! Wild boars get so big that some hunters use dogs and shotguns instead of traditional spears, blowpipes, bows and arrows. The biggest ones could fight off a pair of clouded leopards and they are top predators in the rainforest!'

Amy and George were glad to see Rigu's reaction but asked him *not* to mention it in front of Izzy because the incident had upset her. It made them feel luckier than ever to have got away with only a few ant bites. If hunters needed guns and dogs, what chance would a pair of twelve-year-olds have had?

'I think we should head back, we've been gone for some time. They'll be wondering where we are,' said Rigu.

They moseyed back having enjoyed their afternoon with Rigu. On the way, Rigu explained why they build longhouses on stilts. It was to protect the family against floods and wild animals whilst also sheltering the domestic animals from strong sunshine or rain.

Amy and George felt better having walked off lunch. The rice wine, mountains of food and bugs were now a distant memory. Izzy was a superb guide but the children had enjoyed being with someone closer to their own age. Amy thought Rigu acted and looked older than his age. It was not just that he was the oldest of six children living together but that he had learnt so much. He did not have the advantage of school yet he could hunt, speak a foreign language and barter for goods using the carvings he made with his own hands. He had acquired so many skills for his age. Amy only hoped that one day she could speak any foreign language as fluently as him.

Her mind was racing with new thoughts and ideas. Since she started this adventure a whole new world had opened up before her. What is alien in one country is the norm in another. People in England think they cannot survive without their car, dishwasher, washing

117

machine and personal knick-knacks but here, you had to learn completely different skills to survive. Tribes hunted and planted seeds to grow food for their families; not just to make money but to survive. They had little or no access to the Internet, so world news generally came by word of mouth. They had to hunt for animals or keep and feed them. Everyone at home bought meat from the supermarket without a second thought. Would people back home pluck chickens or be prepared to kill their own lunch?

What if Rigu came to Colchester and visited the pond in the park with a few birds and hardly any trees. He would hate the choking exhaust fumes from the thousands of cars, buses and motorbikes racing to beat the traffic lights. What would he think of English schools or the massive local hospital? Amy smiled at the thought of Rigu preparing beans on toast, using their electric tin opener, microwave and jumbo four-slice toaster.

Izzy spied them from the veranda and walked over to meet them. 'Can I borrow these two? I hope they haven't caused you any trouble this afternoon,' she said jovially.

Rigu laughed, 'I could make fine hunters out of this curious pair in no time.' He then told Izzy in Malay that she must have taught them a lot, as they already knew much more than he expected them to.

Amy and George thanked him profusely but Rigu was modest and said he knew little compared to his father. He was just glad that they were not bored.

Izzy waited until Rigu had walked off, 'I've spoken to Terangu about my plan but I wanted to run it past you.

I'm still very worried about the missing monkeys and the bizarre goings-on, especially as some have happened near our lodge. What I'm getting at is this, would either of you mind if I went back to the lodge for a day or two to try and get this mystery solved? I'd sleep here tonight and then leave you with the family from tomorrow morning. I know I'm meant to be with you all the time you're here but ... I just don't want any more close scrapes when we head back to the lodge, I'd never forgive myself. What do you think?' said Izzy hesitantly.

They looked at each other and for a change George said nothing. As Amy had won this holiday, he was happy to follow her decision, 'I think I can safely speak for both us. Whatever you're doing is in our best interest. We'll be happy here if today is anything to go by. If Terangu can teach us one hundredth of what Rigu knows then we're in good hands. You don't have to worry about us, we'll be fine,' enthused Amy trying to convince Izzy.

'Is it okay with you, George?' asked Izzy.

'Well if it's okay with Her Majesty, then it's cool with me ... *but* will we still get to use the blowpipes if you're not around?' asked George, his mind already on tomorrow.

'I think you'll be pleasantly surprised by tomorrow's activities so don't worry your heads about that. You won't even notice I'm not here,' replied Izzy.

The gong was bonged once more and it echoed across the clearing. Startled birds took flight from the nearby trees. 'Before we go back for dinner we've one question for you Izzy? It's slightly embarrassing,' said George.

'What's troubling you Captain?'

'The toilet doesn't have a flush. You squat down over this hole and put your feet on either side. That part was okay but a little tricky on the first attempt. Did I do the right thing by using the water in the small plastic bucket to throw down the hole and then the water in the large bucket to wash my hands?' asked George.

'By the sounds of things, you got it spot on. They have squat toilets throughout the Middle East and in many Asian countries. I've been to many restaurants that have squat toilets, except they have a little hose to wash yourself down. You get used to them but I prefer the western ones like at the lodge. I should've told you sooner but it didn't cross my mind,' replied Izzy.

'Well George, we're certainly experiencing new things today. We've bought our first pig, given him away, drunk some foul tasting rice wine, eaten crickets and cockroaches, learnt how to trap pigs plus how to use a squat toilet. Not bad for a day's work!' declared Amy.

'It's not over yet, we don't know what's for dinner, spider surprise?' replied George, only half in jest.

Izzy took them by the hands and they happily ambled back to the longhouse for dinner. She was pleased to see how much they looked out for each other, like brother and sister rather than best friends. They enjoyed a much simpler meal than lunch with no surprises. It was a quieter affair because the grandparents looked rather hung-over and the nephews and nieces had eaten before everyone else.

The children asked Terangu loads of questions but his standard response was, 'I'll show you in good time, my young friends.' Most of the questions related to local flora and fauna so they realised they must be going out in search of more wildlife.

Terangu did tell them that his family practised a religion called 'Animism': this meant that every single thing in the universe is alive and has emotions and feelings. He explained this included rocks, stones, plants, trees and animals plus everything else. The children thought this rather quirky as the family loved eating chickens and wild pigs. He told them that as long as you showed respect to all of your surroundings, it was still okay to cut down the odd tree to build a house for your family or breed chickens so you could one day eat them. The family grew or made things and were never wasteful. They lived in harmony with their environment.

He was not sure they had understood, so he continued, 'The rainforest is a large community, an ecosystem, where everyone has different jobs so they can live together. Some animals are predators, so they have to eat other animals to survive and if they didn't there would be problems. If the leopard suddenly said, 'I don't want to eat rats or deer anymore. I'm going to eat fruit like the monkeys'. What would happen next? The rats would eat more and more; then breed until the whole rainforest was filled with rats. If there were too many rats for even the snakes to eat, then other animals would starve because the rats were eating their share of the food. The mouse deer would breed and breed with no leopards to eat them and would strip the rainforest of all the vegetation. The monkeys and the birds would have less fruit because the leopard wanted a change. If one part of the rainforest family does not do its job, it affects everyone. We think of ourselves as part of the rainforest family, our religion follows this.'

Amy and George nodded in agreement as it slowly began to make sense. If one generation after another of the same tribe or family was to live in one part of the rainforest, then it was sensible to care for *all* of their surroundings. This is another reason why people cutting down trees, polluting rivers and poaching animals affected everyone.

'That's enough questions for this evening. Call the children in and we can show you some traditional dances,' said Terangu.

The nephews, nieces and Terangu's boys put on their robes as Izzy began to explain, 'All tribes have a large number of dances performed for funerals, harvest time, welcoming ceremonies, a child's birth or any number of reasons. The Iban tribe have a dance involving the male warriors using the extraordinary strength of their teeth. They dance whilst holding a stone on a cord weighing around twenty kilograms from their teeth.'

The thought of this made Amy and George wince. It gave George a feeling similar to someone scraping fingernails down a blackboard. Amy's teeth were on edge at the thought of someone dancing whilst holding something heavier than the monitor lizard they saw, between their jaws.

Terangu appeared with an instrument that looked like a xylophone. He placed it on the floor near Amy and George. By the time he made a few more trips, he had assembled enough instruments for their own mini-orchestra. Terangu had removed a few gongs from the wall and hung them from a wooden rack in front of where he was seated.

'These gongs are family heirlooms. We don't just use them to call guests for dinner but as instruments for ceremonies and as a warning system. If we had a fire or an enemy attacked, although we have no enemies anymore, then someone would strike the gong. It would wake everyone up or bring them running back here,' said Terangu.

'I think you'd wake the dead if you struck the largest gong with all your might Terangu,' said George.

The grandparents were seated nearby with small, tambourine-like instruments at the ready. Pantai's sister was going to play a small wooden nose flute, which caused Amy and George great discomfort as they tried desperately hard not to laugh.

George whispered to Amy, 'I hope she hasn't got a runny nose or this could get messy!'

Amy and George were given animal hide kettledrums that were shaped like egg timers. Pantai pulled the wooden style xylophone or 'Jatung utang' towards her to play. Terangu came over and showed them how to hold the drums so they gave off the loudest, clearest echoing drum beat. Terangu tapped two sets of simple beats for them. George had to play da-da-dum, da-da-dum while Amy played, dum-da-dum, dum-da-dum.

Terangu gave the signal to Rigu and he came forward and addressed the family in Malay, then English, 'The Datun Julud is a welcome dance normally performed by girls but all the young ones wanted to do it together as a way of welcoming our guests.'

The grandparents kicked off with a few shakes, Terangu followed with a few light strokes of the gongs. Pantai on the xylophone and her sister on nose flute were the next to join in before Terangu gave Amy and George the nod.

The children were light on their feet and danced as gracefully as ballerinas. They looked quite professional and had obviously practised this routine many times, moving in time to the different instruments. With the younger children being unable to communicate with Amy and George, this was an even more special greeting. Amy and George kept up their beats until after everyone else had fallen silent but no one minded those few extra drumbeats. Both guests cheered and clapped loudest of all.

The dancers bowed their heads before quickly disappearing behind the partition. Terangu tapped out their next two drumbeats, when Rigu raised his spear with both hands they must stop. When Tema raised his spear with both hands they were to start playing again. The six younger members of the family had barely been 'backstage' for a few minutes when they reappeared with different headgear, necklaces and both Terangu's boys were carrying deadly spears as tall as either Amy or George. They realised Izzy was missing from the happy throng and must be behind the partition helping them get changed.

'Professional bunch this,' said George, 'they even have their own props and costume assistant!'

Once more the grandparents started shaking their instruments before anyone could explain what the dance was called. Everyone else followed suit but very quietly at first. It took Amy and George no time to realise what this dance was; hunters about to go into the rainforest. It was half dance, half pantomime where the older boys portrayed themselves as stealthy hunters - which was not hard to believe.

Rigu completed another circuit before raising his spear in both hands and letting out a Tarzan-like roar. The hunters stopped moving and the nose flute was the only instrument playing which built up the atmosphere. The nose flute alone sounded particularly haunting. The dance showed them drawing near the prey; the grandparents began to softly shake their tambourines. The instruments were played with more speed and volume now as the dance quickened. Tema raised his spear in both hands so Amy and George started drumming again. The young ones were jumping and leaping around as if possessed by an evil spirit. The wild dance ended when Terangu struck the largest gong just as the two hunters were about to set upon their young prey.

Amy and George broke out into spontaneous applause, 'What a show!' bellowed George.

Izzy came out from behind the partition, clapping enthusiastically. Terangu explained they also had dances for everyday jobs like making sago flour or pounding rice. The nephews and nieces milked the applause before heading off to bed. The grandparents went off to the veranda for a quick puff of old stinky before they retired to bed.

Amy and George were glad they lit scented bark on the veranda because it smelt of lemons, lessened the stench of the homemade cigars and kept the mosquitoes away. Amy and George soon said goodnight and headed to bed, whilst Izzy had a final chat with Terangu. The children were exhausted and soon sound asleep under the roof of a tribal longhouse.

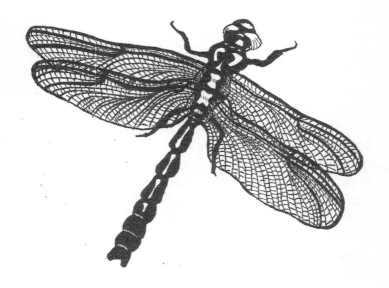

CHAPTER ELEVEN

The enormous fiery, reddish orange sun arose that morning and the rainforest alarm clock began with a vengeance. Amy and George were awake in a jiffy. If their parents had tried to get them up at this unearthly hour, it would have been pillows over the head time and loud groans from both. Izzy knocked lightly and then came in to open the wooden hatch. It was not just the buzz of insects or cawing of the early birds that caught her attention; she gestured for the children to come and take a peek. They crawled out from under their mosquito nets and peered into the rainforest. A golden haired long tail macaque was happily eating berries without a care in the world. The sun reflected off his coat and made him look majestic. Silkier, smoother and more dazzling than any monkey they had ever seen. Amy thought this handsome monkey looked simply splendid in the morning sunlight. Another macaque could be heard chattering and howling, the regal looking monkey slowly headed off into the thicker part of the rainforest to seek out his raucous buddy. The children went to wash and brush their teeth whilst Izzy packed ready to head off to the lodge that morning.

Later on, Tema called them for breakfast where they enjoyed Izzy's favourite fruit called 'Lichi, Lici or Litchi' depending where you were from in Malaysia. They had spiky durians and herbal tea to wash it down. Amy and George enjoyed the sweet tasting durians but understood why local hotels had banned the fruit. The durians give off a strong aroma that has a habit of lingering. The 'rambutan' as they were also known, looked unappealing and hairy. Once you peeled off the outer layers, the acid sweet taste of the delectable inner pulp that surrounds the seeds was worth the wait. Pantai had got the boys up early to catch and prepare Izzy's much-loved breakfast.

Rigu and Tema had bagged some fresh, plump dragonflies. They had been steamed over the cooking pot, mixed with coconut flesh and wrapped in banana leaves. This was poles-apart from Amy's usual bowl of 'Choco-Snaps' cereal. Alarm bells began to ring as everyone else tucked in, so Amy and George had to take the plunge. They could not really savour the dragonfly because of the strong taste of the coconut. Once the top of the pot was cleared of all the steamed surprises, the next breakfast platter was served.

Inside the pot was a smaller pot with even larger dragonflies, longer than George's index finger, which had been boiled in water, coconut milk and ginger. These long thin squishy insects tasted like the inside of a melted bounty bar mixed with a sprinkling of a crunchy ginger nut biscuit. Both children tucked in with relish. At this point, when they would have happily settled for herbal tea or seconds of fruit, Terangu got up from the table and lifted the heavy cooking pot off the stand. There was something left on the hot coals.

'Oh marvellous,' thought Amy, 'whatever next?'

The largest dragonflies of all had been roasting on the hot coals during breakfast. Terangu got Rigu to serve these prehistoric monsters, legs, wings and all to the guests. George thought of offering his to Pantai as a small thank you for cooking breakfast but realised it might offend the hosts. The words *dragon* and *fly* never had such meaning to both children. The dragonflies' wingspan was larger than a human hand-span.

'You can eat the wings as well. They are lovely and crispy after being roasted over the hot coals. Excellent, flame grilled dragonfly. What a treat!' said Izzy.

'Thanks, Rigu, for getting up early to catch these,' said Amy politely.

'Thanks, Tema. It's kind of you both to go to so much trouble,' added George, who was first to bite into one. He bit the head off and then plucked a wing, popping it in his mouth. Funnily enough, he enjoyed it. He thought it tasted like something from one of Tom's barbecues. It had a slightly charcoal flavour that needed a bit of liquid to ease it down the throat but was not bad. George added the word 'bagus' meaning good or nice, which his hosts appreciated.

Amy thought hers was too salty, too crunchy and tasted like old tree bark, but she still managed a smile.

Once they had all finished, Izzy said a few words in Malay to thank the family for their hospitality and for agreeing to look after Amy and George. She finally thanked the two boys for her breakfast. When they all left the table, Amy and George went to help Izzy to load her things into the boat.

'I know you'll have a brilliant time but make sure you keep writing your journals and taking photographs. The family will teach you new skills while I'm away so enjoy yourselves. Hopefully, I should have this mystery solved in a day,' said Izzy.

'Don't worry, we're in safe hands. I bet those rascal monkeys have found a new quieter home and you'll be back in no time,' said Amy encouragingly.

'Take care Izzy and don't forget about us!' said George.

'I'll be back before you realise I'm gone,' stated Izzy matter-of-factly. She gave them a joint bear hug, hopped into her boat, flashed them a smile and was gone. Once she was out of sight, they both felt a slight pang of nervousness because she had been with them throughout the trip and they felt safe with her by their side. Amy knew their parents would be horrified if they ever found out that they had been left alone with a tribal family having known them only one day.

They headed back and came across Rigu and Terangu who were hanging round pieces of wood from the branches of a tree. They noticed that the pieces of wood had circles clearly marked on them and looked suspiciously like targets. George's heart began to race; his pulse quickened. He was dying to try a traditional hunter's blowpipe. What twelve year old would not want to fire darts using this handy weapon?

'We knew you'd be sad to see Izzy leave, so this should cheer you up. We can teach you a traditional part of our culture, the blowpipe,' said Terangu.

Rigu came across and whispered to them, 'Izzy made us promise we wouldn't use any poison tip darts!'

Terangu brought out three different length blowpipes for them to try. As soon as Amy saw the largest one, she knew she would not be able to hold it steady. The largest one was roughly two metres in length and had a small sharp spear attached to one end. This one was covered with an eye-catching carved motif.

'Did you carve this blowpipe Rigu?' asked George.

'Not this one. This has been passed down from one generation to the next, so one day Terangu will pass it to me and I'll pass it down to my son.'

'Yes,' confirmed Terangu, 'It's the family blowpipe and an heirloom only passed down when the father dies. He's the oldest, so when I die it's his job to protect the family so he'll inherit the blowpipe.'

'This has not been used for a long time, so we thought it was worth trying. If you can hit the target with this, you can hit it with anything,' commented Rigu.

Terangu brought out what looked like a coat rack; a tall piece of wood with a base and pegs sticking out from it. He told them the blowpipe would be too heavy to hold for any length of time so they should rest it on one of the pegs.

'You must master the blowing technique, as it's the most important part of firing a dart,' said Terangu.

'Who is to go first,' asked Rigu.

George was chomping at the bit to get started but remembered his manners, 'Amy first.'

Terangu rested the blowpipe on one of the pegs and passed the blowing end to Amy to hold. There was a small notch of wood sticking out at the very end of the blowpipe, which acted as a sight. The spear was on the underside and the sight was on the topside of the blowpipe similar to those on old-fashioned rifles. Terangu told her to look down the blowpipe and use the sight to aim where she wanted to fire the dart. He showed them the darts and asked why they would have a piece of softwood attached to the end of each dart.

'I suppose it would help the dart to go in a straight line, like the end of an arrow does,' answered George.

'A good start,' replied Terangu. 'If the dart is blown out, using the full force of one breath it also needs to fit snugly inside the blowpipe. Then all of your breath is used to force the dart out of the blowpipe.' He popped the dart in for her, a perfect fit with no gaps around the edges. 'Amy, purse your lips a little, as if you are about to whistle. Take a deep breath before putting your lips to the end of the blowpipe. Then force your breath out from the very bottom of your lungs, as quickly and powerfully as you can!' Terangu let out a short, sharp but energetic breath to show her how to do it.

Amy pursed her lips and took a deep gulp of air and followed Terangu's instructions to the letter, emptying her little lungs in a fraction of a second. The dart arrowed from the end of the blowpipe and made a satisfying whistle before piercing the outer edge of the target.

'Top shot, Amy!' exclaimed George, moving closer to the target to examine his friend's fine first effort.

'You certainly have a lot of puff,' said Rigu.

Amy was trying to hide her delight because she had been afraid of embarrassing herself. She thought the dart would fall lamely out of the end of the blowpipe having travelled barely a metre or two.

George was up next and he had a few practice breaths to get the feel of how it was done, especially now under pressure due to Amy's good form. He slightly adjusted the blowpipe and took careful aim at the same target. George exhaled with all his might and fired the dart just outside the central ring of the target.

'Good shootin' Tex!' called out Amy, as she went forward to see just how good it was.

'I think we have a couple of naturals here,' admitted Rigu.

Terangu and Rigu both fired their darts but were only just inside the mark set by George. Terangu went and hung up the ceremonial blowpipe in the longhouse before rejoining them.

Amy and George then practised with the ninety centimetre blowpipe and the one metre twenty blowpipe. They found it much more difficult when not using the coat rack to support them. A tiny gust of wind, a lack of concentration, a shake of the arm or even aiming for too long made it near impossible to hit the target. For two hours they tried their best but soon found out that the shorter, lighter one was much easier to handle. Rigu left the three of them so he could finish off some carvings before heading downriver tomorrow with his brother and uncle.

Terangu admired their efforts and suggested a competition between them, just for fun. 'Whenever we go out in the boat we pick up any rubbish we see, whether it is old fishing nets, soft drinks cans or plastic bottles. People throw stuff in the river not knowing or caring that it pollutes the animals' habitat. All these things can be used over and over again. I don't think some of my countrymen, or yours, realise the earth cannot provide for us forever unless we help her out occasionally.'

Terangu withdrew sixteen soft drink cans from a large bag of river rubbish. He nimbly climbed up a nearby tree, and placed the cans on different branches at various heights. He came back to mark a line for the competitors to stand behind. Amy and George were hoping to hit about four out of the eight cans because they were a good distance away.

'So, whoever hits the most cans wins. Good luck Amy,' said George.

A gust of wind blew and toppled two of the cans. George ran to replace them in the tree, as he was eager to get started. It took him longer than expected because he was laughing so hard.

'What are you up to? Have you stuck those cans down with chewing gum or something?' rebuked Amy.

'No, but that would've been funny. I've been reading the labels! I thought these cans would be cola or lemonade but they've some weird fizzy pop out here; *'Big Mamma's traditional root beer'* and my personal favourite is *'KickaPoo Joy Juice*, for all your energy needs". Saying the name again out loud, made George laugh even harder than before.

Amy laughed and snorted in a very unladylike fashion. Terangu had no idea what they found so funny and it took some minutes before Amy stopped laughing long enough to tell him. 'Back home, 'KickaPoo Joy Juice' would go down a storm. That's definitely the funniest name for a soft drink ever!'

It took them a full five minutes before they could regain any sort of self-control. Once they had got the giggles out of their systems, George offered Amy the first shot.

'After finding 'KickaPoo Joy Juice' you go first George.'

Trying to be a good sport, George aimed for the highest and trickiest can. After aiming and a few seconds of silence, he fired his dart with arrow-like precision knocking the can to the ground. Amy chose the easiest can because she wanted to keep the score even and not let George get an early lead. Amy's first dart struck its intended target and the can fell the short distance to the floor. The sound of the dart striking the can was very satisfying to the two young marksmen. The pair discharged their darts with faultless accuracy until Amy's sixth dart missed its target, due to a slight twitch of her arm muscle.

George hit another difficult one to maintain his perfect record, now seven out of seven. Amy lined up her next dart very carefully but fortune was not on her side. As she exhaled a freak gust of wind swirled across their homemade shooting range sending Amy's dart high into the tree. Silence was all they expected to hear but something unexpectedly thudded to the ground. Amy could not look so George and Terangu went to check it out.

'Well, the rainforest has brought you some lunch. That gust of wind also caught out this squirrel,' admitted Terangu.

Amy felt awful, terrible in fact. She was no killer or at least she did not mean to be on this occasion. George acted instantly to cheer her up, 'Terangu, what predators feed on squirrels around here?'

'Snakes, raptors and clouded leopards are a few who would gladly dine on a plump squirrel like this.'

'Amy, you've probably done him a favour. Imagine if a hawk swooped down and grasped the squirrel using its razor-sharp claws. This way was painless compared to being ripped apart by a ravenous raptor and having your insides eaten,' said George persuasively.

'I felt better at the word hawk… but thanks for the vivid description,' joked Amy.

'If you two finish up here and then have a break before lunch, I'll go and give this to Pantai so she can roast it on the fire.'

Amy's heart was not in her final shot having seen George polish off his eighth can in a row. After missing, she congratulated George and they collected up the cans before heading back to the long house for a rest.

Lunch was a small affair because everyone was off doing little jobs. The grandparents were teaching the youngsters how to make headdresses, necklaces, belts and bracelets with small beads. Rigu was working on his carvings. Pantai had been pounding rice before cooking lunch and the others had been out collecting firewood in large homemade baskets strapped to their heads and shoulders.

The one new dish was roasted squirrel and as Amy pointed out, 'It does taste just like chicken.' They finished off their sticky rice and squirrel before ending the meal with fresh fruit and herbal tea.

'I thought we should make use of the Perahu canoe this afternoon because Rigu, Tema and my brother-in-law will be taking it early tomorrow morning. I'd like to catch some fish so we can prepare a nice dinner. Then, after dinner, we can go look for civets in the rainforest. Izzy told me you had not seen any on your previous treks,' suggested Terangu.

'Amy might know from her animal books what a civet is but I've no idea,' admitted George.

'I think it's a mammal related to a mongoose but I can't remember what they look like,' answered Amy.

'Civets are nocturnal, good climbers and have very sharp claws,' added Terangu.

'I can't wait! It sounds intriguing,' said George.

'What do we need to bring with us for fishing, Terangu?' asked Amy.

'You need your old clothes and drinking water. Izzy asked me to remind you to put on hats and sun lotion. You can get burnt even when it's cloudy in this country.' Amy and George went off to change.

'Amy, can a mongoose really kill a king cobra? And do you think these civets can too?'

'I'm not sure about civets but the mongoose definitely wins once in a while. It makes its fur stand on end so it looks larger to the cobra than it really is. Then it does a little dance until the snake strikes. If the snake misses, then the mongoose bites it behind the neck and wins, but if the cobra doesn't miss then it's bye-bye Mr Mongoose.'

'That's awesome! Birds that eat snakes; giant snakes that eat boars; wild boars so big they can fight off leopards; clouded leopards that take on orangutans and civets; plus the mighty mongoose that isn't afraid of a deadly cobra. The fact animals have to eat to survive makes the animal kingdom so interesting; it always leads to these curious animal duels. The vegetarians and small prey have to work so hard. They are always trying to escape, confuse, fool or hide from the top predators! It's magical here, thanks again for the invite buddy,' said George, who was having the time of his life.

'I'm glad you're having a great time. It's terrific to have good company, especially so far away from home,' answered Amy cheerfully.

CHAPTER TWELVE

They got ready and went off to the canoe to meet Terangu for a relaxing afternoon's fishing. Terangu was putting a few things in the canoe but the children could not see fishing rods anywhere.

'Are we using hand lines with hooks, Terangu?' asked George, intrigued, as he had been fishing with his dad a few times.

'Well, I have one just in case you two don't have any luck with these!' he said, raising two spears above his head having pulled them from inside the canoe.

'Spear fishing!' gasped Amy, who had never held a rod and reel, let alone a spear.

'I thought I'd teach you a traditional way to fish in shallower streams, using these bamboo spears,' explained Terangu.

The spears were roughly a metre in length and had sharp points at the end, ready to skewer the fish like the egrets did with their beaks. They pushed off from the bank and Terangu used the long pole to guide them towards a much shallower and clearer section of the tributary.

'You must be sensible and take care with these,' warned Terangu in a firm but friendly manner. 'You have to stand up when using them and in this canoe that takes a lot of balance. If you feel yourself falling in, throw the spear away because, being bamboo, it floats so we can easily get it back.'

They went along the tributary until they reached a part where the trees were set further back and the water was transparent in the bright sun. Amy realised the benefits of the canoe, which, because of its flat bottom, could glide down the shallowest streams. Izzy's boat would not have been able to get to where they were now. Terangu put down his pole and asked the children to move so that they were at opposite ends of the canoe.

'Now just stand up and make sure you've got your feet securely planted and you're properly balanced.' He let them get settled in their positions and used to the boat's gentle movements. 'Are you both okay?'

'Yep, fine thanks,' replied Amy.

George agreed tentatively with a nod of the head.

Terangu passed them the thin, sharp pointed bamboo spears. 'This involves having a great deal of patience and can be rather hit and miss.' He did not mean the pun but it made them both laugh.

Patience is not a virtue normally associated with children but Amy and George did not mind. The sun was shining; the water was clear, the birds were singing and they were learning an ancient tradition. Both took time to get used to the weight of the spear and the short, sharp, striking movements required. They struck at shadows for an hour or two before their confidence grew. Soon the pair learnt not to make wild jabs and they listened carefully for when they heard the other strike. Amy almost bagged her first fish after George had narrowly missed with his strike; as the fish then swum into her strike zone.

Terangu taught them about other fish in Borneo including his favourite, the archerfish. It shoots water at insects on overhanging branches, spitting water like a bullet and knocking them into the water where they can be swiftly devoured.

After a few hours, Terangu put his baited hand line over the side of the long wooden canoe and this helped to attract more fish. Suddenly, with the speed of a javelin thrower, Amy had struck and this time the end of her spear was not empty.

'Good catch,' said George, 'but what the heck is it?'

'It's a type of catfish, you can tell by the whiskers coming from the upper jaw,' replied Terangu. 'One more like that would be marvellous'.

It was quite smooth and scale-less, shimmering under the sunlight, also appearing to change colour as Terangu handled it.

The catch gave them renewed energy, so after a drink they went on into the late afternoon. In this time, Terangu caught a couple using the hand line but threw them back as they were too small. He told them about a catfish he once saw that looked like glass; you could see its insides.

'There is another method of spear fishing. Hunters stand very still in the clear and shallow water. Once they've been in the water for some time, the fish don't notice them any more. Then bang, one quick strike and they can go eat!'

Terangu eventually caught enough fish to ensure a good supper for the family but suddenly the canoe began to rock.

'Woah there,' said George, as he struggled to regain his balance after a lighting strike.

He used his spear as if balancing on a circus high wire and the rocking almost toppled Amy over as well.

'Good work George, but you almost sent me overboard,' teased Amy, who could see he was lucky to have stayed upright himself.

Terangu removed the dead silvery-green catfish fish and weighing it in his hands said, 'It's just shorter than the first one but much fatter and weighs more. Well done!'

George's face, already rosy from having caught the sun, glowed with pride at the praise for his catch using this new skill.

'We can go back and treat my family to a fish dinner. You two children would cope very well in the wild, if you set your minds to it.'

'Thanks to you Terangu, we might last a bit longer but I think the leopards, venomous snakes and wild boars would still give us some trouble,' laughed Amy.

'Don't worry about that. If Izzy isn't back soon, I will show you how to tell which animals have come and gone by recognizing their tracks and the signs they leave behind,' replied Terangu.

The happy trio made their way back to the longhouse. Pantai was glad to see their haul knowing none of the fish would go to waste. She boiled up the fish bones and skin in her cooking pot just as she did when they ate chicken. Once it had boiled for a while, she removed the bones and had enough fish stock to make soup. Pantai was shocked to find out that not many people in England bothered with homemade soups. She thought it a terrible waste to throw away chicken and fish bones, when with a little effort you could make a wonderful soup. Amy and George did not want to let them know what a wasteful, throwaway society they lived in. They dared not tell her about microwave meals designed by scientists that contained so many additives and preservatives.

The children had been impressed by how little this family could live on, whilst not affecting the environment around them. They grew vegetables; they never over-fished; they patched up old clothes and did not waste a scrap of food. They kept their animals in good condition and made things to barter or swap for other provisions. This tribal family could teach the average family in England a thing or two. The children felt they had learnt so much already; they would definitely encourage more recycling as soon as they got home.

At dinner, Rigu thanked the children for using their new skills to provide the fish. He thought they were bound to have good luck tomorrow selling their goods at a local market. The children said he would not need luck. They were positive he would have no trouble selling or bartering with them, if the carvings were anything like the ones they had already seen.

While they were eating dinner, Terangu told them that he hoped for rain during the evening to make tracking easier. After Amy and George had eaten their fill, they fed the pig and put on their leech socks ready for the trek into the rainforest. The predicted rain came just as they were about to set off. Amy and George nipped back for their thin waterproofs and to spray on some more mosquito repellent.

'Do you want some mosquito spray Terangu?'

'No thanks George. They don't trouble me as much. It may be something we eat or the bark that we burn at night. The mosquitoes certainly prefer people from foreign shores.'

With their torches at the ready, they set off behind Terangu who was carrying a small lantern. They did not think his light was at all useful because it only gave off a dim glow. Amy and George soon realised that he probably did not need much light, as he knew his way around instinctively. The crickets, cicadas and frogs were noisier than ever. Their communication with each other, echoed throughout the forest like the bird and monkey calls did during the day.

Upon spotting light reflecting back from an animal's eyes, Terangu stopped them and pointed high up into the branches. The light beams from the children's torches settled upon a Buffy Fish-owl.

'You can recognise this owl by the distinctive feathers around its eyes,' he murmured. 'The sharp beak is good for ripping apart prey like fish, mice, frogs, small rats and anything else it can snatch up in its claws.'

'You've got to love that bird's bushy eye brows,' whispered George.

'Yep, they're pretty distinctive. It's just a shame we don't have a camera good enough to get a photograph,' replied Amy.

The light rain stopped and the moon was escaping from behind the last clouds, helping to light their way.

Terangu gave them a hand signal to follow him quietly down the trail. Amy and George trailed close behind him for ages until they noticed he was no longer just ahead of them. They had completely lost sight of Terangu. Panic set in, they were alone in a rainforest with leopards, bats, spiders, snakes and wild boars for company. They did not even have spears or blowpipes to protect themselves!

It does not matter whether it's losing your mother in a supermarket, becoming separated from your uncle at the fairground or experiencing the elevator doors closing before your parents got in: suddenly being alone brought a wave of fear for both children. They held hands and edged forward much slower and more cautiously than when they could see Terangu in front of them. The canopy of treetops let in more and more moonlight up ahead but there was still no sign of Terangu. Just as they were contemplating calling his name, Amy saw a dim light swinging from side to side about fifteen metres away just above a line of low shrubs and bushes.

'That has to be Terangu signalling to us?' said Amy hopefully.

'He must have found those sneaky civets,' whispered George, thankfully.

Amy pointed her torch towards the ground so she would not trip over and alert these nocturnal animals to their presence. Making their way towards the faint light ahead, they carefully crept forward trying not to tread on any loose twigs or debris on the forest floor.

They caught up with Terangu who was peering over the shrubs into a small moonlit clearing. The children switched off their torches and took a peek. Scuttling around were two surprising animals. They looked like cats or large ferrets; they had a mongoose nose with whiskers like a cat and a patterned body. George later told Amy he thought the smaller one looked a bit like a raccoon.

The animals were aware of one another's presence, whenever they got too close one would let out a half growl and the other would hiss and shiver slightly. After observing them for a while, Amy and George guessed they were either looking for food or marking their territory. It was easy to lose sight of them in the moonlight because they both had first-class camouflage. The larger civet, which Terangu told them was a Malay civet, had a spotted coat that looked striped at times as it blended in with the trees. The smaller stockier one had a darker, fuller, coat with a slightly smaller snout and could disappear in and out of the shadows at will. The civets' claws must have been very sharp as they climbed up and down the trees as if they were still on flat land. Amy's attention had been diverted by a rustling on the forest floor amongst the fallen leaves. She covered her torch with her hand so it only let out a tiny amount of light. The civets were carnivores and liked to eat a variety of small animals. Amy braced herself in case it was a mouse trying to get away from these attractive but deadly civets.

George and Terangu were engrossed in the civets' performance and because their eyes were now used to the moonlight, they could see more of what was unfolding. The large eyed predators were searching for food like eggs, fruit, small mammals and frogs. The civets also did not want to give ground to one another. Later that evening, Terangu told the children that the civets have to be very careful. If they make too much of a commotion when disputing territory, sharp claws or not, a leopard or panther might find them and they would become its dinner.

Amy finally caught sight of was causing the rustling noises; it was a worm-tailed black rat trying to escape unnoticed from the area. Before she had a chance to tell George, a long, mean-looking snake came out of the shrub that he was crouched behind. The rat was now far too close to George's leg. Amy could not let the snake strike at its prey. What if the snake was venomous and it missed its quarry? George would not get the anti-venom in time. The nearest hospital must be over four hours away from this spot deep in the rainforest. Her instincts took over. Amy switched off the torch and removed her hand from the end of it. She steadied herself because any misjudgement could prove fatal for either her or George.

Amy struck cobra-like and seized the snake with a pinch grip behind its head. The rat ran, the snake hissed, George turned and let out a yelp of horror as he toppled backwards. The civets disappeared into the night in a blink of the eye.

'Amy. We'll move behind you and then you release the snake at the bottom of the shrubs and jump out of the way,' said Terangu calmly.

Amy waited for them to move to safety. Then as quickly as she could, she released the snake onto the soft ground where it had appeared.

'Gadzooks, that was close. I think I've just wet myself,' said an ashen-faced George.

'What type of snake is it, Terangu?' asked Amy, no longer alarmed as everyone was out of harm's way.

Terangu took the torch and shone the light onto the green snake to confirm his fears. 'Sorry George, I bet that gave you a fright! I should've realised the civets would have driven all the rodents away from the tree. It's a venomous Pope's pit viper, sometimes called a tree viper. You can identify it by its triangular shaped head and smooth head scales. It has fangs to inject venom into prey like rats, frogs, birds or lizards.'

'What would have happened if it had bitten me, Terangu?' asked George, trying to sound calm. Although his heart was still pounding like a drum, after this close escape.

'I'm not sure. Children who get bitten would be affected much more than adults. I've seen an adult bitten by one; as well as serious swelling around the bite mark itself, he had severe pain in his arms. The bite was sore for quite some time. However, the snake would not want to waste its venom on us. It can see how big and hot we are, so would bite only out of self-defence and then slip away into the night.'

'What do you mean it would see how hot we are?' asked George.

'I'll tell you on the way back to the longhouse but I think we should leave this snake to catch some dinner and stop disturbing the civets.'

As they trailed behind Terangu, George quietly said to Amy, 'That could have been bad if it had sunk its fangs into me, whether deliberately or by accident. I owe you one buddy!'

'Don't thank me, thank Steve Irwin. I saw it on one of his old TV shows.'

'What a legend! Who says you can't learn anything from watching TV?' replied a relieved George.

'Anyway, you saved me from being crushed to death by those hunger-crazed boars, so that makes us about quits!'

On the walk back, Terangu apologised again for not being careful enough. When he saw the palm civet and the larger Malay civet he was captivated. He enjoyed watching their behaviour and seeing how they reacted to each other.

'It's not your fault Terangu. George is back to his normal chatty self and no harm has been done,' said Amy, trying to reassure him.

Terangu was obviously still upset as the children were his responsibility. 'The rat was trying to get away from either the sharp claws of the civet or the fangs of the snake'.

The children tried to cheer him up by keeping him occupied with a multitude of animal questions. Terangu went on to explain that civets have retractable claws, so they do not wear them out too quickly. If they wanted to climb a tree or scratch around for fruit they would unfold them. If they were silently looking for prey they would keep them safely folded up. He also told them about a coffee that you could make from civet dung. One type of local civet fed on coffee cherries; you could sift through the civet faeces and extract the partially digested berries. This can then be used to make a blend of coffee. Terangu thought this the most normal practise in the world and was surprised to see the look on their faces.

Neither liked coffee but they were both disgusted to hear about this exotic dung coffee.

This tale had left George with an awful taste in his mouth, so he repeated his question from earlier, 'What did you mean when you said the snake could see how big and hot we are?'

'This viper has a special organ on its head which acts like one of our human senses. This pit organ allows the snake to identify and see its prey using their body heat. That is how it's able to tell the difference between a rat, a bird or, possibly, a human,' replied Terangu.

He promised to answer their questions the next day about how bats see in the dark and how large rats can grow but first they needed a good night's sleep.

They arrived back at the longhouse and thanked Terangu for such a spellbinding day before quietly slipping off to their quarters. After brushing their teeth, they pulled out their mosquito nets and got inside. They fell asleep before even wishing each other 'goodnight'.

CHAPTER

THIRTEEN

The rain pattering on the longhouse roof woke the children from their peaceful slumber.

Amy pushed aside her mosquito net, gave a big yawn and opened the wooden shutters. 'I hope the weather clears up. It will be horrible for Rigu and the others going to market today if it stays like this.'

'But it might help us! According to Terangu, light rain will make finding the animal tracks easier. Still it's a bit strange, I would have thought it washed any tracks away but I guess we'll just have to wait and see,' replied George.

'Let's get washed and see if Rigu needs a hand,' suggested Amy.

By the time they were ready, the rain had stopped and the clouds were beginning to drift apart. They had barely gone ten metres when Tema called to them from under the longhouse.

'What's in here?' asked George, as he offered Tema a hand with some bags.

'Bead necklaces, bracelets and other stuff the family has made. We'll try to sell or swap these at the market,' replied Tema.

Rigu turned up just after George and Tema had gone to load up the canoes.

'Good morning Rigu,' said Amy.

'It is a good morning but I'm sad that you and George will leave once Izzy gets back.'

'Don't worry, we can send you letters. We'll post them to Izzy; I'm sure she won't mind dropping them in from time to time.'

'Before you leave, can you write down your address and phone numbers for me please?' requested Rigu.

'Of course, but why our phone numbers?' asked Amy, a little puzzled.

'Well, if you can keep a secret . . . one of the men who buys my carvings wants to trade me an old mobile phone. It would be much easier for him to contact me and tell me what figures and statues he needs. He sells them to tourists in other parts of the country for more money but he's always been fair with me when bartering.'

'But how will you charge it?'

'He'll give me two fully charged batteries. He says if I keep the phone switched off at night then they last a lot longer. I will then give the batteries back to him or to Izzy to charge up for me,' replied Rigu, who had thought of everything.

'That's great but what will your dad say about all this modernisation? Whatever next, a computer or satellite television?'

'When he sees how much it will help the family if I sell more carvings, he'll see that a phone has advantages and won't complain . . . I hope!' said Rigu.

'Oh, I nearly forgot!' he added. 'Be careful when you put on your shoes, I've seen a few scorpions around here. They enjoy hiding in warm, dry places and don't like being disturbed.'

'Where did you find them?' asked Amy.

'One large one was between two of my carvings and I saw another couple when I was working. I must have woken the big one up because he raised his stinging tail at me and clicked his pincers.'

'But... but what did you do with all of them?' remarked Amy, having only ever seen one from behind the glass in a vivarium.

'I herded them onto some wood and moved them away from the house. I didn't want the younger ones getting stung. A sting from a scorpion is painful but they would be more scared of us than we are of them; the same with most animals in the rainforest,' explained Rigu.

'That was brave; I'd have been terrified!'

'Once you know how to deal with them, there is no need to be scared,' declared Rigu reassuringly.

For the rest of the morning, Amy and George chatted and helped the boys and their uncle pack, unpack, and repack the canoes. Pantai brought down fruit and bowls of fish soup that she had prepared from the leftovers, having realised that everyone was too busy for breakfast. Terangu had not been seen much that morning and was acting in a clandestine fashion.

By the time everything was loaded, there was little room left for passengers. The other canoe had less on it because it was going to carry Tema and his uncle as well.

Terangu re-appeared as everyone gathered on the bank to wish the boys well at the market. He addressed Amy and George, 'We wanted to give you these when Izzy was around but because she's not back yet, the boys asked me to do it now before they go to market. Thank you both for the pig and catching the fish for last night's feast. It's good for us to have young visitors to come and live with us.'

He handed Amy and then George a thirty centimetre tribal blowpipe, hand-made by Terangu with motifs carved on each by Rigu. Each blowpipe had a different set of animals and insects carved onto it. They were much lighter and far easier to handle than even the smallest of the blowpipes that they had previously used.

The children were ecstatic and for a few seconds at least, speechless. They did manage to find a few adjectives to describe their presents – amazing, excellent, incredible, wonderful and fantastic were but a few.

'Terima kasih banyak - thank you very much!' they exclaimed with beaming smiles.

Amy and George wished Rigu, Tema and their uncle a safe trip to the market. Amy gave them a hug and promised to keep in touch using Izzy as the post-woman. The canoes set off slowly from the bank and they were soon out of sight. The children's happiness evaporated and gave way to a feeling of gloom as they had become so fond of Rigu and Tema.

Terangu put an arm around their shoulders and led them to where they learnt to shoot the day before, 'I've made a few darts for you both to use but if Izzy has not returned by tomorrow morning, I'll show you how to make them. You will have to use different materials to replace these darts when you get home. Make them well and they will do a good job.'

'I'm sure she's en-route but if Izzy isn't back, can I learn how to make necklaces with Pantai while you teach George how to make the darts? That way we each learn something different and can share what we've learnt when we get home.'

'I'm sure Pantai would be delighted to show you. We'll just have to wait and see what time Izzy turns up,' answered Terangu.

Amy and George practised with their custom-made blowpipes until they stopped for lunch. Terangu had bored out the centres of the blowpipes so smoothly and expertly that the children rarely missed. They laughed when they noticed that Rigu had carved a squirrel onto Amy's blowpipe. Rigu had engraved cockroaches, crickets, dragonflies, wild boars and other creatures along the length of each blowpipe. The children were overjoyed with their unique gifts and really felt as if they were part of this tribal family.

After another appetizing meal, Amy and George prepared themselves for a trip into a different part of the rainforest. They assembled leech socks, water, cameras, waterproof jackets, comfortable walking shoes and fruit. Having sprayed mosquito repellent on their hands and necks, they were ready to go. They went outside in search of Terangu and found him with a woven mat strapped to his back.

He saw their quizzical expressions, 'If we need to kneel or crouch down to observe any animals, we'll put this down and it will help us all to see fire ants, spiders or any rats fleeing from venomous snakes. We'll be looking at animal tracks on the forest floor so this should also keep you a bit drier.'

'We trust you Terangu,' said George, who was keen to avoid any more deadly snakes.

'We know we're in safe hands,' added Amy.

'So far this trip you've been animal spotting. This is different; today you're going to learn how to track animals. You must promise to use these skills wisely to help animals. You must never disturb them or affect their habitat. If you scare parents away then the young may be abandoned and die. Be careful never to damage feeding areas or disturb any nesting grounds. What I'm going to teach you is a *gift* to be respected,' said Terangu, in a serious but fatherly way.

'I, Amy Applegate, promise to use what I learn today to help animals.'

'I swear by the Cooke family name to abide by these sacred rules,' said George earnestly.

'If poachers learned some of the things I'm going to show you, the animals would have even less chance of survival,' said Terangu in a gentler tone.

They set off slowly into the rainforest but before long Terangu signalled for them to stop, 'Have a look around, try not to move your feet too much. Look high, look low, be observant and in a minute tell me what you can see that might lead us to an animal.'

The children studied as much of the surroundings and forest floor as they could from where they stood. They both crouched down to look at the lower bushes, as well as the nearby trees.

'So, children, what does this area tell you about the local habitat?'

Amy went first, 'Well, maybe the broken twigs on the path were actually broken by a monkey or large bird. I can only see tiny marks on the floor which could be birds hopping along. These birds are far too small to have broken the twigs, so they could have just been looking for food.'

'A good start,' encouraged Terangu. 'George, what do you think?'

'There's a strange smell underneath the bush which could be an animal marking its territory. There's also a small amount of poo over there. From a quick glance it looks like the lead of a pencil so it might be a small mammal. Maybe a mouse or a baby rat,' answered George. Their local guides' knowledge and love of animals was starting to rub off on George as well.

Terangu was impressed; this area was popular with rodents because it offered many places to hide in the undergrowth. If a predator, like a raptor came along, it could perch on the branches above and use its sharp eyes to spot its prey. The small bird prints showed that they had been feeding on the loose berries that were dropped by the monkeys high above.

'Animal excrement can tell us which animals have been here and when. The size, colour, smell and content of the excrement plus the nearby tracks, give a good idea of what animals are around,' said Terangu.

'I know the poo isn't made by a rabbit,' said George, 'because it doesn't look like *M&M sweets*!'

Terangu was unsure what George meant so took a closer look.

'A young rat did those and there may be quite a few nearby, we should carry on looking for more spoors further into the rainforest.'

'Two questions please, Terangu,' asked Amy. 'What is a spoor and how big can rats get in the rainforest?'

'A spoor is any type of track or trace an animal has made or left behind whilst it moves around. It could be a footprint; a scent given off to mark their territory or attract a partner; even debris like the broken twigs we saw. It includes animal's faeces or excrement, whichever you prefer to call it. Now are you sure you want me to tell you about the rats?' asked Terangu with a smile.

'I have to know how big they get,' answered Amy, 'because at least then I'm better prepared if we came across another one. I was fine with the one I saw yesterday but it was only a tiddler.'

'I've seen a rat which was this big.' Terangu held his hands about thirty centimetres apart. 'The body and head would be as long as your blowpipes. The tail could be another twenty five centimetres long. They have self-sharpening teeth and, unlike lizards such as geckos, if they lose their tails in a fight or to a predator, it's gone for good! It cannot grow back or regenerate.'

'That rat would be as big as our pet cat. I wouldn't mind having a pet rat if it grew to that size. It would help keep away the nosey neighbours,' said George, half in jest.

'George, your Mum would have a fit if you came home with a pet rat!'

They carried on walking until Terangu stopped them, 'What could teeth tell us about an animal?'

'A bite mark could tell you what type of shark had bitten a surfer,' said George, who had recently seen an

Australian on the news who survived a horrific shark attack.

'If the plants were cut like scissors, then you would know it was not a deer but a rat or something else with sharp pointed teeth,' remarked Amy.

'Why would it not be a deer?' questioned George.

'Deer pull grass and plants up from the ground. Just like cows, they graze on vegetation and then chew and chew and chew! They have flatter, less sharp teeth to help them to chew their food,' said Amy, happy that information from her books was coming in handy.

'Well done! Bones and animal remains are helpful in finding out what has been in the area. Some rodents gnaw at bones for the calcium, which in turn keeps their bones and teeth strong. If you find an animal carcass, you could tell what attacked it by measuring the bite marks. If you found a bone with saliva and teeth marks on it, you would know a predator was nearby because wild dogs often go back to chew the bones for the nutrients,' said Terangu.

They kept on walking, only stopping briefly for fruit and water breaks. The children took numerous photographs of birds, hornet's nests and monkeys in the canopy. Amy and George took it in turns to write brief notes, so they did not waste any tracking time.

They trekked for a while longer before Amy pointed to a large heap of earth, 'What's that Terangu?'

'That's a termite mound and a great tool for tracking animals. Take care where you're walking because you may step on other animal prints. Look around and then tell me what you think.'

They searched around the mound in an orderly clockwise fashion, so as not to miss any clues. They caught sight of a small termite and could tell it instantly from the ants they had seen because its head was so much larger.

'He must have led us here for a reason. Even two amateurs like us could not have missed this giant termite mound,' said George.

'Everything in the rainforest eats something else, so what eats termites?' replied Amy.

They spotted what could have been tracks leading to the other side of the mound. An animal had clearly tried to claw its way in to get an easy dinner. They placed the woven mat down and began to examine the prints and the hole. Amy took out her note-pad and began to sketch the tracks when George noticed something.

'I think we might be trying to find two different animals. The print there, looks like three fat fingers but the one you're drawing looks like a lion's paw or something with claws,' exclaimed George, getting excited.

As soon as Amy had finished the two sketches, they had another brief look around before rejoining Terangu.

'What animals have you unearthed, children?'

'We're positive animals are coming here to feed on the termites because there are scratch marks and a hole. We also found a set of paw prints, right near the first tracks,' said Amy.

'We can't identify the animals, however if this was an ant hill, I would have guessed that one of the sets of tracks was an ant-eater,' added George.

'I'm glad I brought you here,' said Terangu, 'you've done well in solving this mystery. In Malaysia we have an endangered species called a pangolin. Its name comes from the Malay word meaning 'roll-over'. It's also known as the scaly ant-eater and it loves ants and termites.'

'Well done, George!' said Amy, impressed at his powers of deduction.

'The pangolin digs into the mounds with its powerful front legs. It has a sticky tongue that can extend a long way into a hole. All the nearby termites get stuck and it pulls in its tongue with dinner attached. It can also roll up into an armoured ball, covered in its hard protective shell and roll away, hence its Malay name. Its other defence is a scent gland that can give off an awful smell.'

'Like a skunk,' said Amy. It was Terangu's turn to look baffled, so Amy continued. 'The American skunk is a mammal that fires chemicals from its anal scent glands. The glands produce an unpleasant sulphur smell of rotten eggs or burnt rubber.'

Terangu did not want to track this animal any further because he had seen the tracks of a young pangolin. He did not want the female to become aggressive and wanted the children to find out more about the first prints they had found.

'I'm standing by this tree to give you a clue to the identity of the owner of the paw print,' teased Terangu.

Both children had been so engrossed they had not noticed any other animal spoors.

They looked around the tree until George said, 'If these scratch marks on the tree trunk are claw marks, then we might be looking for a bear. It could have been sharpening its claws or trying to climb the tree. Are there any bears in Borneo and what would they eat?' He was thinking that maybe they ate honey like '*Winnie The Pooh*' but he kept this to himself, as he did not want to sound stupid.

'Do you think the world's smallest bear, the sun bear, might be the correct answer?' said Terangu.

'Sherlock George strikes back,' quipped Amy playfully, 'these tracking lessons are certainly paying off!'

'I think you should both be proud of how quickly you're learning about the rainforest.'

'Our Mums keep telling us that our brains are like sponges, so we should absorb all the info we can whilst we're young,' said Amy.

'My memory is definitely not a sponge, it's more like a sieve!' added George with a shrug of the shoulders.

Terangu told them that the sun bear was around one metre tall and ate fruit, lizards, termites, worms and honey. George cursed to himself for not mentioning honey, he had been told by his teacher never to be afraid to put up his hand up. Better to offer up a sensible suggestion or idea than to stay quiet.

Amy and George were learning about more than just animals this holiday. They were learning about themselves and each other; lessons that would prove valuable in years to come. They continued trekking through the rainforest which was full to the brim with wonderful animals and insects. It was not long before they came across another important member of the rainforest ecosystem.

'Children, here is the famous dung beetle with his ball of animal dung at the ready. This beetle would fight long and hard if another male tried to steal it,' said Terangu.

'Why would they fight over dung?' asked George.

'Women of course,' answered Terangu with a smile. 'For the male to attract a female beetle he must offer her a ball of dung. Not the nicest wedding present but it's practical for starting a family. The male beetles have strong limbs; their front limbs for digging holes and fighting other males, their back limbs are super strong to be able to push these heavy balls of dung. One male beetle can roll and bury a dung ball over 200 times his own body weight. Once he has fought off the other males, collected his dung, dug his hole and found his beautiful beetle wife, then they are ready to begin mating. The egg hatches underground and the larva burrow into the dung ball. It keeps warm and well fed until it pupates and bites its way to freedom.'

'But why is this so important for tracking, Terangu?' asked George, wondering where this was leading.

'This beetle follows the scent of mammals; it knows where to find dung. The dung beetle can lead you to other animals. They also have wings and fly upwind towards the scent. These beetles, like worms, fungi and bacteria, are a vital part of the rainforest ecosystem. They are known as 'decomposers' and help break down the dung so the soil gets the goodness back. Having good soil means plants, trees and vegetation can grow more easily,' explained Terangu.

'It's wonderful how every living thing in here is linked to everything else. The smallest ant is linked to the largest tree and so on,' said Amy, amazed at the interconnecting wonders surrounding them.

It was getting late in the day so Terangu suggested they use this clue to track one last animal before it got too dark. He explained that a lot of animals preferred to come out when the sun was beginning to go down.

'What animal will this dung beetle lead us to?' asked George.

Terangu examined the dung ball closely and then had a good long sniff, 'This dung is made up from mostly animal faeces. That animal was eating large amounts of fruit and seeds, so we are now looking for hoof prints.'

'Horses! In the rainforest?' queried a puzzled Amy.

'Not a horse but a distant relation. The animal is a mammal called a tapir and most people think it's related to a pig, an anteater or even an elephant. It's more closely related to a horse or rhinoceros than any of them.'

'This sounds like another weird and wonderful animal, but what does it look like?' enquired Amy.

'I won't spoil the surprise, just wait and see. We must be quiet because this is a solitary animal that likes eating and avoiding predators,' replied Terangu.

'What does the tapir hoof print look like?' asked George.

'The front legs have four toes and the back legs have three. It makes quite an impression on the soft floor because they are stocky animals. It brushes against low bushes, trees and small branches, so you need to look out for broken twigs near the edges of the trail. Be watchful near areas that would give good cover, thick tangles of vegetation or anywhere it could push through to escape from a predator,' answered Terangu.

As they searched for clues the noise overhead increased; it was a high-pitched squeaking sound changing rapidly from close by to far off. The children were concentrating on the forest floor for tracks and had not noticed an increasing amount of winged company. The high-pitch sound made them turn around and look up. Instantly, they dived to the ground to avoid being struck in the face. Two bats soared low and swooped for a flying insect, barely missing the children.

Terangu tried hard to stifle his laughter, when he saw them hit the deck so dramatically.

'They won't crash into you, even if it was pitch-black and you stood there without torches. These bats have tiny eyes and big ears but can navigate this rainforest at night better than anything else. They give off a sound which helps them to locate trees, insects, and their surroundings; even young children! The sound bounces off an object and when they hear the echo, they locate exactly where they are and what's around them.'

'Is it the same way dolphins find their way around underwater? A type of animal sonar system?' asked Amy, whilst lying on her stomach in the dirt.

'Izzy told me that dolphins, as well as bats, use forms of echo-location. Listen to how the sound changes when they get near an insect,' said Terangu.

He picked up a small stick and crouched down, as the children were both still on the floor. When the bat flew past he drew three lines in the soil, spaced equally apart. They listened and the beeps became more rapid, so Terangu drew nine lines in three groups of three. Within seconds the sonar beeps were incredibly fast, indicating it was close to its prey. Terangu drew eighteen lines very close together. The bat snapped up its meal and then returned to making regular high pitched beeping sounds. He drew another three lines on the ground exactly the same as the first set and explained, 'This is the bat searching around' - pointing to the first three lines, 'this is the bat approaching the insect' - he pointed to the three groups of three lines, 'this is just before the bat gets his meal. The bat then makes lots of little noises to get a final, accurate picture of the insect from the returning echoes.'

George pointed to the bottom line, 'This is the bat going back out for dessert?'

Terangu nodded, while Amy smiled and said, 'Do we still have time to find the tapir because the light is fading fast?'

'If we work quickly to find the hoof prints, we should be okay,' said Terangu, striding off down the trail.

Amy and George smiled at each other as they got up from the forest floor. They both had muddy hands and faces and looked in a real state but neither of them cared in the slightest. Who doesn't enjoy getting dirty once in a while?

After a further twenty minutes searching, Terangu motioned for them and pointed to a shrub next to a tree and whispered, 'This is where the tapir crossed the trail and went deeper into the trees. If you shine your torch here, you'll see squirrel prints. The squirrel jumped from here, back onto the tree trunk to avoid the tapir that was trundling by. The prints are smaller at the front and bigger at the back, so the squirrel jumped up to get away. The shrub is damaged and there are rub marks on the bark of this trunk. The animal is accidentally smoothing down this part of the tree trunk and pointing us in the right direction.'

'You could be an animal detective! We'd never have seen that in a million years. We were concentrating so hard on finding the hoof prints that we missed all these signs,' said Amy softly.

'In time you would pick it up, especially if you lived here. It's taken me a lifetime to watch and learn these techniques. Remember children, practise in the rainforest at home and you'll be experts in no time.'

They did not want to correct Terangu but exploring the rainforest in England would be impossible. Practising in the local wood looking for badgers, moles and voles would have to suffice.

After a fruit and water break, they left the trail and headed silently into the thickest part of the rainforest. The children were glad they packed both torches, as they certainly needed them now. They followed closely behind Terangu but the quieter they tried to be, the noisier they thought they were. The cicadas were raucous that evening, so it helped to mask the sound of the children's footsteps. Terangu finally struck gold, as there were fresh faeces ahead. It was mushy and had a potent pong but this did not deter Terangu from examining it closely. The children were glad it was not them poking through the poo!

'The tapir has been feeding on soft, fresh fruit and berries. We're very close, look around and tell me what you see.'

Amy and George knew Terangu well enough by now, to know when he was giving them a hefty clue.

They moved their torches over the rainforest floor to inspect the fallen leaves. They quickly spotted leaves that looked as if they had been compressed into the dirt. Amy and George removed the leaves in these places first and soon found a four-toed hoof print and a three-toed hoof print. After finding the other two prints, they now had the full set of four pointing them in the right direction.

'If we had more time, we could measure the hoof prints and the distance between them to estimate the tapir's height, length and weight. However, I want to find the animal quickly because we're still a distance away from the longhouse,' explained Terangu.

They followed the direction the hoof prints pointed to and eventually came across another set of prints. These prints were in softer ground and Terangu noticed something odd about them, 'We must be silent! It has an injured leg and will damage it further if we frighten it.'

Being a life-long tracker, Terangu now knew exactly where to head in order to get a glimpse of this rare creature. He led them on until he heard the snuffle and snaffle of the tapir rooting for food on the rainforest floor. He put his finger to his lips and pointed upwards; he helped Amy and then George into the closest tree, although he did not follow them up.

They looked on in astonishment and silent admiration at this exceptional animal. It had a black front, a white rear, a fat, stocky body similar to a pig but with an extraordinary proboscis snout. The snout was not as thin as an anteater's or as long as the trunk of an elephant but it was truly unique. It used this snout, joined to its upper lip, to browse around a leafy area on the rainforest floor. When it found a nice berry it would grab it and put it straight in its mouth. They could only marvel at an animal most people would only ever see in a book or a zoo. Even then, that would not match the bizarre beauty of watching this rare Malaysian tapir in its natural habitat.

About ten minutes had passed when George put his hand over Amy's mouth and pointed to another tree, maybe twenty metres away. What she saw almost made her shout out to scare away the injured tapir. Some type of large cat, a leopard or panther, was working its way around the tree line. They did not want this predator to be alerted to their whereabouts but they also did not want the tapir to become the cat's supper. Upon closer inspection, it had two main stripes along its back and dark round markings. Sometimes its patterned coat looked spotted and sometimes it looked one colour. Its superb camouflage helped it blend in with the surroundings. It was a chunky predator around a metre in length.

George was making hand signals to get Amy's attention. He wanted to get down, to look for Terangu, as he was no longer beneath the tree.

Amy shook her head! She had no intention of letting him get out of the tree with another dangerous creature within spitting distance. She whispered in his ear, 'Better for us if it has the tapir for dinner, rather than attacking you. When Terangu returns we'll jump down and ask him what to do.'

'Agreed, but that tapir is easy game with its bad leg,' replied George faintly.

Amy did not want to see the tapir get hurt but she did not want George to get mauled either. A rustling of leaves close to the tapir made it stumble off painfully, getting closer to the hidden hunter with every step. The children could not look away; it was like a natural history documentary unfolding in front of their very eyes.

Amy heard a soft birdcall. Terangu was below them and signalling for her to climb down. She quietly got down but George kept watching, mesmerised. He should not have because he saw the predator leap, ambushing the tapir from its hiding spot. It jumped onto the tapir's back, holding on with its razor sharp claws. Its strong legs and huge clawed paws helped it keep hold. George took one final glance and saw the huge cat bare its teeth and sink them into the tapir.

George bolted down the tree; their escape went unnoticed due to the commotion nearby. Terangu swiftly moved them away before they heard the death cries echoing around the rainforest, as another predator caught its prey. Later on, Terangu estimated that the rare clouded leopard weighed about twenty kilograms. It had the largest teeth for its weight of any of the cat family. Its large cutting incisors were ideal for thick hides like deer, boar, pig or a tapir.

No one said a word until they were half way home when George finally spoke up, 'Don't you think we should have tried to help it, maybe fixed its leg or something?'

'One of the main forms of defence a tapir has, is its ability to run. It is a strong and fast runner that can crash through thick undergrowth to escape from a predator. With an injured leg it wouldn't last long in the rainforest. This was the natural way, it continues the cycle of life. The tapir would not only be dinner for the clouded leopard but mice, birds and rats might also get a nibble. Then it would decompose with the help of worms, beetles and return to the soil, thus helping other plants to grow,' explained Terangu.

This was of no comfort to George. He had a sneaking suspicion, that something was not right. Although he kept it to himself, he believed that it was Terangu who made the noise which startled the Tapir. Terangu must have seen the leopard and drove the tapir towards it, so no harm came to them. He would not have wanted another incident like the one with the venomous viper. The walk home was a quiet one as the children reviewed in their minds what they had seen and learnt that day: seeing two rare animals with only one surviving the night.

When they arrived back at the longhouse, they left their shoes outside and tiptoed in, not wanting to wake anyone. Pantai was up and having seen the torchlight, she had warmed up some homemade soup for them. It was delicious and greatly appreciated because the temperature had dropped and Amy and George were now feeling the cold.

Another day of the holiday was over and the days were streaking past. Two questions occupied their minds as they went to bed. Was Izzy okay and had she found the missing monkeys? They wished each other goodnight and promptly fell into an exhausted sleep.

CHAPTER
FOURTEEN

Both children woke up feeling stiff after their long trek. They were still sleepy but thought better of going back to bed in case Izzy arrived early on. It looked like being a calm, bright and sunny morning.

After they had got washed and ready for breakfast, Amy said, 'The one problem with having no telephone is that you feel cut-off from the world. I'm with Rigu on this one. If we had a phone we could call Izzy and make sure she was okay. I would be less worried if we had one to hand.'

'I agree with you but it has been cool to get back to nature. No ringing phones, no internet, no *Playstation*, no radio and nothing but wildlife and trees as far as the eye can see. Oh, and some not bad company to share it with!' replied George.

'Not bad? Thanks for the compliment!'

They turned up for breakfast to find Terangu at the table but there was still no sign of Izzy. The food was already waiting so they enjoyed a light meal together.

'George, now we've finished eating we should get started on the darts,' suggested Terangu. 'Once Pantai is ready, she will come and get Amy.' Terangu got up, smiled at Amy and left the room.

George slowly raised his aching frame from the table and went onto the veranda. He popped his head back round, 'Smell you later alligator.'

Amy shrugged her shoulders and sighed, knowing George would never change. As she sat waiting for Pantai a thought crashed into her brain. She leapt to her feet and careered out onto the veranda. 'Hold on George!'

George was down the far end of the veranda, 'Amy, surely you can't be missing me already?'

'Rigu found scorpions around the longhouse, so you should check your shoes.'

'I wouldn't have thought they could handle the smell,' joked George, as he picked up his shoes. He theatrically shook them out onto the veranda, 'See, nothing to worry about.' When he looked down he let out a high-pitched scream and jumped backwards. 'You've got to be kidding me!'

Amy moved forwards and saw him pointing his shoe at a scorpion. Its stinger tail was loaded and ready to defend itself. George had shaken the scorpion from its warm but smelly hiding place and was ready to strike back using his shoe.

'Don't you dare hit it George! We have to move it away from the house,' declared Amy boldly.

George looked at her in utter astonishment, 'No way Jose! Terangu's over there, ask him to move it?'

'No! Rigu told me what to do. The only way for me not to be scared of these arachnids is to do it myself,' replied Amy. She looked around for a long enough piece of wood. It took a while for the scorpion to climb up onto it but eventually it did. George checked Amy's shoes for her and then they went to release it into the rainforest, a safe distance away from the longhouse.

'That was perfect timing, Amy! Looks like you've bailed me out of trouble again.'

'Not really, I should have told you yesterday! What if you had stepped on that scorpion or one yesterday afternoon?'

'But I didn't; so thanks for the warning. Better late than never and that's good enough in my book.' George smiled and winked at her, before heading off to catch up with Terangu.

Once George was out of sight, Amy let out a huge sigh of relief and made a mental note to make sure she always passed on important information immediately.

Both children were pleased to have a chilled-out morning; sitting down for longer than an hour made a pleasant change. Their physical exertions were starting to take there toll on the two children. Amy felt tired but much fitter than she had ever been before.

Pantai turned up soon after and began explaining why the Orang Ulu tribeswomen loved to work with beads. Centuries ago, beads were brought from far off places such as the Middle East, India, China and even from Venice. Sailors brought fashionable antique beads to trade with them. In return, the sailors would receive food supplies or animal hides, important for their long journeys throughout Asia. These beads were used to create distinct patterns on items like sword sheaths, baby-carriers, baskets, ornamental belts and headbands for the tribesmen.

Pantai took down one of the decorative designs from the wall. Amy was astonished by the complicated and elaborate designs created using tiny coloured beads. The striking and colourful pattern must have taken Pantai a great deal of time. Pantai had brought many different boxes of dyed seed beads ready to be made into bracelets and necklaces to sell at the market. It was a slow and painstaking job to pierce holes in the beads and put them on the thread. She was enjoying Amy's company; especially because her two sons preferred carving, hunting and fishing and showed no interest in beads whatsoever.

When Amy finished her first bracelet, Pantai said, 'Please keep it as a reminder of your stay in the longhouse. Although you better make one for George so he does not feel left out.'

'How do you make the dye for the beads?' asked Amy

'It's simple; you boil and grind up different flowers, roots and berries from around the rainforest. Then you add the beads to the dye and leave them,' replied Pantai.

'Simple but brilliant,' Amy could now picture how a traditional technique could be handed down from mother to daughter over thousands of years.

Meanwhile, Terangu was showing George how to make a wooden plug that fitted snugly into the end of his blowpipe. This hard plug acted as a size guideline for all the dart ends. All George had to do was shave the softwood ends using his hardwood plug as a guide. George took great pleasure in using his penknife to cut, saw and measure everything to perfection. Terangu was surprised to see so many gadgets on one knife. Once George had shaved a good number of dart ends, he went to get more hardwood and a small axe to cut the shafts of the darts. When there were enough splinters of hardwood, George cut them to the correct length and shaved them to a sharp point. This job proved satisfying for George because now he would never run out of darts when he got back home. He could not wait to teach his Dad how to use his blowpipe. He would go to a car boot sale and buy a second hand dartboard as soon as he got home! Once he sharpened the hardwood darts all he had to do was carefully push them into the softwood and he was finished. He had successfully made his own darts from scratch and was elated. Woodwork had just become fun for him.

'Do you want to go and practise?' asked Terangu

'No thanks, I'd prefer to sit out in the sunshine and make Amy a set of darts.

'That's fine but you'd better check at least one dart, to make sure it flies straight'.

George happily hit the fizzy pop can with the new dart, even though Terangu had put it a long way off. He was quickly becoming an expert with the blowpipe, especially now he had his *own* blowpipe and home-made darts. Once George had completed Amy's set of darts and practised for about an hour Terangu came over with a huge basket.

'Would you mind strapping this on your head and waist and coming with me to collect firewood? After lunch, Pantai wants to show you how to cook sticky rice in bamboo over a fire,' said Terangu.

'No problem, but can you help strap it to my head, please?'

Terangu strapped the basket to his head. George found it tricky to maintain his balance but got used to it and began collecting wood. He could bend down and pick up smaller branches, placing them in his head basket. The fuller and heavier it got, the harder it became to carry. When the basket was full, the novelty had worn off and George felt weary. It was as if someone had strapped a concrete block to his head.

When Terangu and George arrived back at the longhouse, Amy was waiting on the veranda. She had her camera in hand, 'Smile George, my little wood-gathering tribesman!'

On cue, George flashed Amy a cheesy smile.

There was still time before lunch so they wrote notes in their journals on this morning's activities. George took some time to draw a stylish 'A' on each dart before he gave them to Amy, who was chuffed with her present. Amy's offering of a colourful tribal bracelet went down well with George. The children already had their bags packed and were keeping an eye out for Izzy's imminent arrival. They were getting more anxious as the time ticked by and still there was no news.

The grandparents, nephew and nieces all sat down to lunch with Amy and George. Pantai had cooked some of the children's favourites including vegetable spring rolls. They enjoyed the nourishing lunch but were looking forward to making the fire. They were not pyromaniacs but who could resist a big bonfire? Flames that leap into the night, crackling wood, smouldering embers and a warmth that makes the skin tingle. Bonfire night at Amy's house was an excuse for her Dad to have a barbecue party. Tom, being the self-proclaimed 'king of the barbecues' would serve his guests an animal burger. It was a double cheeseburger, bacon, egg, gammon, onions plus all the trimmings. Amy's thoughts began to wander; this was the longest time she had ever been away from her family. If her best friend had not come, it would have been awful to choose which parent escorted her on this holiday. That would have been too much, even for a girl who was no longer afraid of bats, snakes and now scorpions.

After lunch and a soothing sit-down in the sun, Amy and George began preparing the sticky rice. The children were set to work grinding and crushing the flesh from inside the ripe coconuts. They pounded, mashed and mixed it with water until it was like glue. Finally adding the long rice grains and mixing them together. Terangu took them outside to a scorched patch of land where they would build the fire.

'Please build a small wooden frame using these three pieces of wood. Use the climbing plants from the rainforest, the lianas, as makeshift ropes to tie the wooden frame together.' He then passed them the hollowed out bamboo that they would stuff with sticky rice and rest on the frame at a 45 degree angle.

After Amy and George had successfully built the wooden frame, they fixed it into the ground behind the fire. The frame would now not get burnt down as soon as they lit the dry twigs and branches. They both took turns rapidly rubbing a small stick backwards and forwards between the palms of their hands into a small woodblock to create hot embers, which could then be used to light the fire. This technique was exceedingly difficult and something the children would need to practise in the future in order to master it. Eventually they used dry grass and matches to light it, after failing with Terangu's traditional method.

Amy and George took the hollowed out bamboo to Pantai and enjoyed getting messy filling it with sticky rice. They went back to the fire and placed the bamboo on the edge of the ground, resting one end on their makeshift wooden goal. To George it looked as if they had built a firetrap, but Terangu reassured them that as long as they turned the bamboo it would cook the rice properly.

He brought them a mat to sit on and a basket in case they ran short on twigs and branches. The children were then left to look after the fire. It was not just the rice that was cooking; they were roasting in the scorching sun. George had to go and get their suntan lotion, hats and water. The children had enjoyed the extra days here but wondered if their new skills would be of any use in a typical English household.

They chatted away all afternoon enjoying each other's company. In all this time together, rarely had there been a cross word exchanged. This was helped by the organised activities; when you are physically shattered you do not have the energy to argue. Under normal circumstances, even these best of friends had the odd falling-out or disagreement. It was only natural.

Terangu popped out now and then to check on them, but they had it under control. They made the odd trip for firewood but took it at an easy pace, so as not to break into a sweat. Occasionally Pantai brought them out some strange fruit slices to quench their thirst.

Terangu and Pantai came out again late afternoon; there was another job he needed a hand with. 'Pantai's father has a sore eye and her mother is, well, blocked up. I'm not sure of the word,' said Terangu.

'Constipated,' replied George, with a wry smile.

'To help with their ailments I have to collect berries, flowers and herbs to make a natural medicine. Would you come and help me? It's only a short walk as I know you're tired today,' said Terangu.

'If Pantai doesn't mind turning the rice, it would be great to stretch our legs before dinner,' agreed Amy.

Pantai took over the final phase of rice duty whilst Amy and George followed behind Terangu. En-route he explained more, 'Most medicines were originally made from plants, seeds, berries or even fungi. In the rainforest it's possible to find natural cures for sore throats or eyes; laxatives to relieve blockages, herbs to help a cold and many more.'

He led them to a patch of herbs, 'Amy, could you pick the leaves from this one here so we can boil them up and that should help Grandma. George, the leaves over there that have the fine hairs and feel smooth can be turned into a powder or liquid to help her sleep. While you collect them, I'll be down here getting red berries to make a paste for Grandpa's eye.'

Before long they had collected enough for some extra doses, just in case the problems persisted. George thought it was time for a risky question, 'Terangu, how do you make poison darts? I mean, if I was starving in the rainforest and wanted to hunt a wild boar but had no spear.'

'I'm not sure if Izzy would want me to tell you.' He thought for a few minutes, 'I suppose it cannot hurt. You are young but responsible, so I will trust you. There are two ways to make a poison mix for a blowpipe dart. One way is to find a Upas tree and make a cut into it, so you can collect the sap. You boil the sap and make it sticky; put the dart tips in it and you have a poison-tipped dart. The important thing is how you prepare it because some Upas tree sap can also be used as a strong flavouring for vegetables. The second way is more dangerous because you would need to collect venom from a snake. To milk the venom we tie thin leaves over a glass jar and then hold the snake behind its head. When it bares its fangs, these are pushed through the leaves and the venom is squeezed out. You would have to take the unharmed snake a long way away before letting it go because it might be a little angry.'

'Thanks Terangu. Your knowledge is safe because I wouldn't go near a venomous snake and we don't have trees like that in England,' said George.

'Your family fish, grow food, breed animals, make beads, carve statues and make poisons and medicines. Over the years your tribe and family have learnt to live without needing more than what's around you. It's *so* different back home. If there's a power-cut all the lights go off and people panic because they cannot find the candles or make a cup of tea. Thanks again for letting us stay, we've learnt heaps,' said Amy, sad that she was soon to be leaving.

Terangu did not know what to say except, 'Thank you.' He was glad to teach them anything he could in the short time they had available. He and Pantai would miss the children when Izzy finally returned to pick them up.

When they arrived back at the longhouse, Pantai had removed the bamboo from above the embers of the fire and was preparing the food. The children washed and changed whilst Terangu went to prepare the medicine.

Dinner was quiet because three of the family were away at the market, two of the grandparents were not drinking rice wine because they felt unwell and the nephews and nieces had already eaten. Over dinner they were taught the local words for some of the animals they had seen: 'babi' was pig, 'musang' was civet and the rare tapir was either the 'chipang' or 'tenok'. George thought tonight's sticky rice was particularly tasty; any food you help to cook always tastes that bit better. They helped clear the table and then sat on the veranda watching the geckos eating bugs and mosquitoes. These fantastic lizards still fascinated Amy and George because of the way they climbed any wall and walked on ceilings as if they were floors. They would sorely miss the geckos and wildlife when they went home. The time came for Amy and George to thank Terangu and Pantai for another rewarding day before departing to bed.

'The less I do the more tired I get,' George joked, before swiftly going to sleep.

Amy settled down inside her mosquito net and was soon swept off to a dramatic wilderness dreamland; very similar to the one just outside the shutters.

CHAPTER FIFTEEN

The children awoke to find a friendly face sitting next to their beds.

'Sorry, I didn't want to wake you up as you looked liked you needed the rest.'

'Izzy! It's great to see you,' exclaimed George.

'We were worried about you!' said Amy, brushing aside her mosquito net and giving her a big hug.

'I know I've been gone too long but it was a catalogue of disasters. After I left here, I got back to the lodge to find the phone was dead and the CB radio was playing up again. I drove to the orangutan rehabilitation centre but my jeep broke down when I was a couple of miles away. I walked the last part and arrived to find a badly injured orangutan had just been brought in. Sati and Nazarus had their hands full trying to save him; I helped them out but stupidly forgot to call the mechanic. By the time all the other orangutans had been fed and the injured one stitched up and sedated, it was night-time. I stayed at the centre waiting for a mechanic to come and fix the jeep. In a way it was lucky because you've learnt a lot of new things and I was able to help nurse the sick orangutan,' said Izzy.

'A few questions,' said Amy. 'Is the jeep fixed? Is the orangutan feeling better and what happened about the missing monkeys?'

'The jeep is fixed,' she replied, 'the orangutan looked better when I saw him late last night, but the proboscis monkeys are still missing. It's because of this, that I want to change the plans for your last couple of days here. We can't contact anyone from the lodge if we stay there and I didn't have time to solve this primate puzzle. I thought maybe we could spend at least one night in another famous cave and then go camping. The other option is spending the remaining nights back at the rehabilitation centre with Nazarus and Sati. They said we could stay there if we wanted to, but it's up to the pair of you.'

'I think we would be doing more good there, than if we visited another cave,' replied Amy. George was overjoyed by this decision, as he was not keen on seeing another cockroach infested cave this holiday. His dreams were bad enough after visiting the last one.

'Well that's settled,' said Izzy. 'Finish packing your bags, get washed and then come for breakfast. Pantai wants to cook for us before we leave. See you shortly.'

Izzy failed to mention that she had helped remove a bullet from the injured orangutan. She thought it best to leave that news until they were at the centre. She wanted them to enjoy one final meal at the longhouse.

Terangu was keen to praise Amy and George; he told Izzy how skilled they had become with their blowpipes, successfully learning the art of spear fishing and dramatically improving their tracking skills. Izzy quickly realised Pantai and Terangu had become fond of them during their stay. She knew this was exactly how she would feel when she took them to the airport.

They had a final breakfast together before putting their bags in the boat. Amy and George were sad because they had loved their time at the longhouse. It had been an eye-opening experience. We will not dwell on the goodbyes because Amy and George still had time left in the day to cheer each other up.

Izzy gave them both leaflets to read as she navigated her way along the small tributary leading back to the Kinabatangan River.

'This is who we'll call when we get to the rehabilitation centre. The National Parks and Wildlife division will have to send some animal enforcement officers to speak to us,' said Izzy.

'How can we help them?' asked Amy.

'We can explain where we saw the proboscis monkey and tell them all the other places we tried but couldn't find any. We could tell them about some of the strange things going on. There may only be as few as one thousand proboscis monkeys left in Sabah and not many more than that in Sarawak. They don't get as much attention as the orangutans so they desperately need our help. If anyone comes to Borneo to make a television programme it's normally about the orangutans and nothing else. This division of the Government *must* try and solve this mystery for us. Those missing monkeys must be found before the mating season starts otherwise it could be catastrophic. If it's foul play, like poachers, then our country has laws to deal with them!' replied Izzy unsympathetically.

George read a bright yellow section of the leaflet aloud:

'Certain wildlife and plant species are totally protected by law in Sabah and Sarawak – Malaysian Borneo. These CANNOT be killed, captured, sold, bought or owned.'

'Does that include the proboscis monkey?' asked Amy.

'Yes, it does. They are only found in Borneo so are a rare and endangered species. Their numbers have been dropping for years due to poaching, trafficking and loss of habitat to palm oil plantations. These monkeys are important for the local ecosystem and economy because they bring in tourists from around the world,' answered Izzy.

Once they were back on the open section of the Kinabatangan River, Izzy said, 'Amy, shall we put on our lifejackets and let Captain George have one final go?'

'Good idea! Us girls can sit here looking for the long-nosed monkeys whilst being chauffeured by the Captain. It's the only way to travel!' replied Amy.

They donned their life jackets and swapped seats. George could not believe his luck, he was as happy as a fox in a chicken house. Izzy was searching one riverbank with her binoculars whilst Amy scoured the other.

They rounded a bend in the river and something caught Amy's eye. A boat was leaving the bank of the river that she had been looking at. It was the largest boat she had seen on the river and Amy hoped it was for tourists and not someone illegally logging the precious trees. When their engine fired up, a dirty thick cloud of smoke spluttered up into the air. 'What a filthy boat,' muttered Amy, 'polluting the local environment.' She was not sure if George had seen it yet because he was concentrating on keeping the boat straight and steady. On closer inspection, Amy noticed that there were numerous crates and boxes on the stern of the boat. She could not tell what the cargo was because it was covered with loose sacks and tarpaulins.

Amy looked at the front of the boat and could not believe her eyes. It was the hulking, menacing man who harassed them at the airport and he was looking straight back at her! She turned to George, 'It's the bully from the airport! He's on that dirty old boat heading this way.'

George had no words to answer and looked worried at this breaking news.

'Slow down to a crawl and turn slightly please George. I want to get a closer look at that vessel,' asked Izzy.

She stood up and looked the boat over. She instantly noticed the gigantic man barking orders to the unseen crew. As the larger boat began to pick up speed, one of the sacks that had been covering the cargo blew clear. What it revealed made Izzy feel sick to the depths of her stomach. A wretched, half starved male proboscis monkey was imprisoned in a tiny cage.

It took a few seconds for Izzy to spit the words out, 'Damn, damn, damn! There's the reason; it's so obvious!'

'What's obvious Izzy?' asked Amy, troubled by her guide's tone.

'They must be the infernal poachers!' she replied harshly.

'I don't mean to worry you Izzy but that boat is certainly not slowing down to a crawl like we have. It's gaining speed and heading straight for us,' exclaimed George.

Izzy let her binoculars fall to the floor as she scrambled to the front of the small boat. She began to wave her arms energetically as if she was doing star jumps. She furiously blew the whistle attached to her lifejacket.

George was not sure whether to turn the small boat to the left or the right as the huge boat drew down on them like a malevolent shadow.

Izzy surprised them both by stopping the whistle blowing and screaming with all her might, 'Turn now! Please turn, there are children onboard!'

'Hold on to something Izzy, they're going to ram us,' cried Amy helplessly.

She was not heard over the increasing noise of the other boat's filthy engine, now running at full pelt. The boat was at point-blank range and it was decision time. George gave it full throttle and accelerated hard to the left at the last second. The junior Captain's manoeuvre certainly stopped their boat from being obliterated.

However, like life, as one problem passes another one rears its head like a cobra from a snake charmer's basket. The large boat may have missed by centimetres but it caused a hefty bow wave that violently rocked and rolled Izzy's small boat.

Before Amy or George knew what was happening their crew was down to two. Izzy had fallen overboard and George was already ten or fifteen metres away, as he had been at full acceleration to get clear of danger. The other boat was slowing and turning back towards Izzy. Amy looked through her binoculars again to see how quickly the boat would turn and saw an even greater threat from the woman with the hook nose.

George slowed and was trying to decide what to do next as Amy screamed to Izzy, 'She's got a rifle! What do we do?'

'GO! Go to Terangu's, NOW! That's AN ORDER!' yelled Izzy, bobbing in the water. George realised that Izzy must have heard Amy or seen the rifle herself. Why else would she order them away? George hesitated for a split second because he thought he might just be able to get back to her in time. He took one last look at the oncoming boat before turning the throttle. He followed Izzy's order and sped away.

To Amy's complete astonishment and horror, each second took them further away from Izzy but also further away from the other boat. She was no coward and screamed at George, 'What the hell are you doing? Turn the boat around!'

'No way,' shouted George, over the noisy motor.

'We *must* help her! Don't you dare leave her George!'

'What can we do against poachers, animal traffickers or whoever they are? They've got guns; we'd be shot, dead! Or captured! Okay?'

Amy and George could no longer look each other in the eye. Their emotions were torturing them. George felt vulnerable, just like Amy, but anger was welling up inside him. The feeling of helplessness brought back memories of being bullied at school. Memories he could do without as he struggled to control the boat at full throttle.

Amy stopped screaming, wiped her tear-stained face and said nothing. This felt so wrong. You do not leave friends behind, whatever the circumstances. She turned her binoculars towards Izzy and could just make out that two of the crew, under orders from Hooknose, were throwing Izzy a rope to pull her onboard. Amy was not the type of person to hate anyone because she had been taught that hate was a destructive emotion. However, Hooknose and the Hulk now topped the list of people she truly hated. Amy was revolted, outraged and frightened all at once but helplessness was the uppermost feeling inside her.

George struggled to control the boat as they careered along at full pelt. They were soon out of rifle range and headed round the bend in the river. He was taking them towards the tributary leading back to the longhouse. As the wind whistled by his head began to clear, he was scared but knew his primary responsibility was to his friends. He did not want to let Amy or Izzy down by not getting them back to Terangu's safely. At least then they could somehow get help. George let the throttle off when they came towards the tributary entrance. He knew that the other boat was far too big to get down a small tributary like this one.

When they arrived back at Terangu's, Amy leapt out of the boat and George threw her the rope to tie them up. Without grabbing their bags they sprinted for the longhouse. Pantai was pounding rice husks with a massive circular pole. The nephews and nieces were feeding the chickens and the pig. The grandparents were busy making bracelets on the veranda and Terangu was inside fetching his tools.

When he saw them running it brought conflicting emotions, delight and panic. Even before the children had stopped running they were both trying to explain what had happened. All he understood from the first few garbled sentences was, 'Quick, quick, we MUST do something!'

'Calm down children! You are both speaking too fast, I can't catch up!' said Terangu.

Again both children began in machine-gun English, far too quickly for poor Terangu to understand.

'Monkey's kidnapped Izzy's poachers! Please children, one at a time, this is making NO sense!' he repeated firmly.

Amy got her breath back so began to explain, 'I spotted a large boat out on the river. On the boat were two people who insulted us and threatened George when we arrived at the airport. They were on the same aeroplane as us from England. The boat came directly towards us and Izzy spotted a monkey in a cage; it was one of the missing long-nosed monkeys that we've been searching for. The boat was going to ram us but George saved us,' exclaimed Amy, stopping so George could continue.

'I only tried to get us out of the way, but the giant boat's wake almost capsized us and Izzy fell overboard. The woman from the airport was on top of their boat with a rifle. Izzy screamed at us to leave and to come here, so that's what we did!'

'We didn't want to leave her but they were coming back for her or us, and they had a gun!' Terangu put his arm around Amy as she finished speaking. She was shaking and had tears welling up in her eyes.

'I know you wouldn't have left if she hadn't told you to. You did the right thing listening to her. She told me how terrible she felt when the boars almost killed you.

She just wanted to keep you safe. What happened next, George?'

'Amy saw them throw her a line and we came back here as quickly as we could!'

'Do you think they followed you?' asked Terangu.

'Not a chance, their boat was much too big to get down here. It would get stuck at the tributary entrance,' replied Amy.

'Was there a small dingy or boat tied to the back of the large boat?'

'I don't know Terangu, it all happened so quickly. Amy, did you see a dingy tied to the back?' asked George.

'There wasn't a boat tied to the back, but they had enough covered crates and cages to have half the rainforest onboard.'

'I must go and speak to Pantai about this while you go and get your bags from the boat. I'll meet you back at the longhouse,' said Terangu before he dashed off.

When they had brought everything back to the house, Amy rummaged through her bags and pulled out her pad and pencils. 'Maybe we can try to piece parts of this puzzle together. It might help us to devise a plan to get Izzy back,' said Amy, desperately wanting something useful to do to take her mind off what awful things Izzy might be going through.

'Somehow, we'll get them back for taking Izzy,' replied George determinedly. They went to the table and began scribbling away in silence.

When Terangu returned, the children looked up at him hopefully, 'Pantai thinks the best plan is for her and her sister to take the grandparents and children to a shelter in the rainforest. We use it on hunting trips for wild boar. She thinks you should go with her as well, I …,' Terangu was not allowed to finish his sentence.

Both Amy and George interrupted him with an explosion of words, 'We're *not* going with them!' 'We can help!' and then adding in chorus, 'We've got to get Izzy back!'

'Hold your tongues please children! What I was about to say, was that I sensed you'd never go along with the sensible plan and would probably refuse to go and hide. I can see now I was right,' said Terangu.

'Sorry Terangu,' answered Amy quietly.

'Sorry,' said George apologetically, looking at the floor.

'No apologies needed. I will tell Pantai to get food and supplies ready for their trip. At least we'll know they are safe, even if the poachers try to come down this way.'

CHAPTER SIXTEEN

On the abominable Ark, Izzy was securely tied up and her hostile hosts were trying to decide what to do with her.

'Should we go after those brats or leave 'em be? What if they find help Ricky? We'll be scuppered!' said Hooknose, whose real name was the entirely inappropriate Lucinda.

'Those two posh brats won't last one night out there, all them dangerous wild animals and no precious know-it-all guide to hold their hands,' sneered Ricky the Hulk, his breath reeking of local liquor and his beer-gut hanging over his belt.

Izzy was trying to say something but could not because of the gag in her mouth.

Hooknose removed this saying, 'Got something useful to say on the situation?'

'If anything bad happens to either of those children, I promise that I'll make you both pay dearly!' said Izzy in an unexpected and menacing tone.

'Ooh! Hark at her. Isn't she brave!' retorted Hooknose mockingly.

'Lady, you ain't in much of a position to be making threats! Sorry but I preferred you with the gag in, back it goes!' scoffed Ricky. 'Let's just stick to the plan. We're almost home and dry. We've got most the list ticked off, except for a few exotic birds and that big cat they discovered out 'ere. We should carry on down river, moor the boat and bag the last few animals. Oh and maybe get a tapir or two if we're lucky. Not a bad plan, eh luv?'

Her nostrils flared like a bull, 'Don't call me luv, you hairy halfwit!' she shrieked.

The hulking poacher shrugged his massive shoulders, wheezing heavily as he lumbered off to inform the crew of their plan. There was no mistaking who wore the trousers in this marriage.

'Much better, thanks,' said Amy, in answer to Terangu's question. Amy and George had now set their hearts on out-smarting these stinking poachers. Terangu had joined them at the table, bringing an old map of the river and its tributaries. The children had made notes on all the irregular goings-on during their holiday.

Terangu opened up the map and the children explained all that had happened. He jotted down the time, date and place of each incident on to the map. This included the puzzling sighting of the entire troop of long-tailed macaque monkeys at the orangutan centre. They marked the most likely places the poachers could have moored the boat in order to scare the monkeys towards the centre. Amy asked Terangu to mark the site where they had seen one solitary proboscis monkey, because Izzy had never seen *any* there before. Then they guessed where the wild boar attack took place. This was also the place where they had found the carrion steaks, almost certainly left by the poachers as a lure for wild animals. Maybe Izzy should have told them at the time that the pig steaks were cut with a serrated knife. She had let them believe that a predator was the culprit.

'What about the men who threw Izzy the rope? What if they were the ones who suddenly didn't show up for work at the palm oil plantation? Izzy said it was normal for workers to disappear if they could get more money elsewhere. She definitely said it was around the time we arrived. The locals didn't know what they were getting themselves into! Hulk and Hooknose must have had to pay very well to keep them quiet about their nefarious plans!' said Amy.

'The bulk of the plantations that are large enough to cope with the loss of two men without thinking much about it are all based around here,' Terangu marked more X's on the map before asking which way the boat was pointing when they first saw it.

Amy drew an arrow on the map, marking the boat's previous direction. Her voice trembled slightly as she added, 'That was before it turned to try and ram us!'

As they were looking at all the arrows, crosses and markings on the map George said, half to himself, 'I wish I had the ancient Asian book that my Dad always has his nose in, The Art of War. It would have helped in a tricky situation like this.'

'What's it about, George?' enquired Amy, who was glad of a minutes respite from making a plan of action.

Her head was throbbing and her heart rate had not gone back normal yet.

'He told me that it could help me take on any playground bullies but I don't think he meant this!' At the time, George had not told his dad he had already fallen prey to the scourge of school bullying. Still, this was not the time for those painful memories to resurface.

'The main parts were about working out your strengths and the enemy's weaknesses. It said to prepare for a short, sudden attack to unbalance your foe. Oh, and there was an excellent part on using spies to get important info about the enemy,' said George enthusiastically.

'Some of that might help but I'm not sure how we'll use spies against them,' replied Amy.

Terangu spoke up, 'We could spy on them *if* we worked out where they've moored their boat. That's if they're not heading straight here!'

Amy and George looked quizzically at him.

Terangu pointed to an area on the map, 'They might stop around here. All the signs are telling us where they started catching the long-nosed monkeys. They scared the macaques and your lone monkey from around here and here, before driving them further downstream. They may have stopped in the rainforest near your lodge to trap wild cats or even a few boars for supplies. Then they could have doubled back upriver for one final sweep. There are many exotic birds along here; a hornbill beak is a good prize for these poachers. Several areas along that section of riverbank are perfect for trapping tapir.'

'Hooknose and the Hulk will find it difficult to blend in with the locals and will want to keep a low profile. It would be tricky to disguise or hide their boat because of its size'.

'Amy you're right; their boat was massive. It would be impossible to hide, especially with a noisy cargo,' said George.

Instantly Terangu thought of two oxbow lakes not far from the area he had initially pointed to, 'These would make perfect hiding places for a large boat filled with noisy, chattering monkeys. The first oxbow lake is a hard three or four hour trek from here.' They continued studying the map and even though this idea had some gaping holes in it, the clues kept pointing them in the same direction.

George was the first to break the silence, 'Well, what are we waiting for, let's go. We've got your best guesstimate, let's try to find them and somehow bust Izzy out!'

'Let's take five minutes to think about what your dad's book said. Firstly, what are our strengths and weaknesses?' said Amy. 'We only have three people and they have four that we know of. They have the advantage of numbers but we may have the element of surprise, *if* we ever find them.'

'We don't know much about them, except that the Hulk will probably have hit the booze again after such a busy day. He stank of booze when he threatened me; he must have been drinking the entire flight,' added George confidently.

'They have at least one rifle and Izzy! This morning they were only poachers and possibly animal traffickers. Without a second thought, they've moved up the *Premier League* of crime by attempting to drown us, sink our boat and kidnap Izzy. So we know they're serious and very dangerous,' admitted Amy in a grave tone.

George nodded his agreement but Terangu had the beginning of an idea. 'I think we'll need a strong brew of the laxative and sleeping draught. I'll go and prepare those now using the leftover herbs and berries from making the grandparents' medicine.'

'What do you have in mind?' asked Amy, intrigued by what he had just said.

'I think we need to use one of our strengths to give us the advantage of numbers. We have two accurate blowpipe shooters here and we could ensure at least one of them has an uncomfortable night. We try to hit one with the sleeping draught and the other with a super strong laxative!'

'It's worth a try. Let's keep our fingers crossed we find them and not have them find us in the meantime. We'll go and pack our rucksacks with the necessaries for the trek,' said Amy. Terangu disappeared and left them to decide what they needed.

There was no animosity between the Amy and George; they would work together because they had a common enemy. Neither friend wanted to mention what had happened between them on the boat. Instead of it dividing them, it had bonded them, uniting them against a couple of scumbags who had crossed the line! They had to save Izzy and try to help the monkeys and any other captured animals.

'Can you put Izzy's binoculars in for Terangu, please George? At least then we'll both have a pair in case of emergencies.'

'You sound like you're expecting trouble, this is going to be a walk in the park!' replied George sarcastically.

'What else do we need except for water, fruit and our blowpipes?'

'Let's wear our darkest clothes, long sleeve tops and baseball caps. It will help us to blend in, our very own type of camouflage. The clothes should also help protect us from the blasted mosquitoes. I think we should change our white cloth leech socks for our long black hiking socks. They are much less visible and should still stop any leeches getting in. We could pull them up over our trousers bottoms and then tie them up with these spare shoe laces my mum packed,' replied George.

'Handy! We'll look like a couple of ninjas from the movies, decked out in black from head to toe. We'd better pack our waterproofs because even if it doesn't rain, they'll help keep us warm when the temperature drops. As my dad always says, 'you can take it off if you're hot but if you don't take it, you'll need it", joked Amy.

'Sounds like good advice. I vote we stick with it because it could be a long, cold night.'

Terangu came back with an armful of extra items. He had his spear, all his blowpipes and a mat, snugly packed into a woven basket that he could carry on his back. 'There were only enough herbs and berries to fill two small bottles; one is filled with the sleeping draught and the other a potent laxative'. He let them inspect the two tiny bottles with corks firmly in place. 'I've brought you both woven cases to keep your darts in and you can use these hardwood pegs to clip the dart cases to your trouser belts. I'll keep the medicine bottles for now, just in case we don't need them. Are you ready to go?' enquired Terangu.

'We'll be ready in a minute, we just need to change our clothes and double check our bags. Please can we take some fruit, Terangu? We'll need the energy for a long walk carrying all this gear,' asked Amy.

He nodded and went off again, leaving Amy and George to get ready for their hopeful but unlikely rescue mission. They were both feeling more and more nervous as the time for leaving drew ever closer.

Although neither had mentioned it, they were both questioning this foolhardy mission. Should they be going to look for Izzy with only three in their party? Should they go to safety with Pantai for a couple of days? What on earth would their parents' have to say about their reckless actions? Were they being stupid by putting themselves into harm's way for a second time today? All these questions and more were racing through the heads of the young adventurers. They both kept coming up with the same answers. Izzy was in trouble and she would never have left them unless she was forced to. They must try to rescue her rather than leave her in the grasp of these odious villains.

'Remember your pen-knife and don't forget your torch either. We may be able to use the torches to signal each other,' said Amy, on the ball as ever.

'Good thinking Bat-girl!' George paused for a second before continuing apprehensively, 'Amy, I've got a sinking feeling in my stomach! It feels like I'm about to sit an exam and have done absolutely no revision. Perhaps it's just a case of the butterflies?'

The questions that were in both of their heads, started to blurt out of his mouth before he could stop himself, 'What if we don't find the boat? What if something goes wrong? What if something happens to one of us, what would the other say to the parents?

What …?' George hesitated, his resolve was crumbling. He was unsure of himself and what he had just said.

'I'm scared too George. You and I both know we can't leave her in the hands of those poachers. There are no police nearby, no army, no navy and no phones to call them with anyway. This is about sticking together, through the good times and the bad. Hopefully, our parents will understand.'

'Or they may not understand and ground us for the next six years?'

'Don't worry, at least if we don't make it back, we won't get grounded,' said Amy, not thinking for once when she opened her mouth.

'Thank you Amy Applegate, but that was not the answer I was looking for!'

'I didn't mean that! We'll be fine, I'm seventy percent sure of that.'

'Well seventy is an 'A' grade, so I can live with that,' added George, trying hard to feel more positive. He knew they would need a lot more than luck to come through this adventure unscathed.

Soon after, Terangu returned with fruit and sticky rice for the trek. They were now ready to go. They walked out of the longhouse and began the trek, Amy soon realised she had forgotten something. She turned and darted back inside, soon after she emerged from the longhouse and jogged to catch them up. This was going to be awfully hard work.

CHAPTER

SEVENTEEN

Wearing layers of dark clothes and the humidity meant Amy and George were perspiring heavily. After an hour and a half they had to stop for a water break to avoid dehydration. Amy laughed at George because a ring of dried, salty, sweat residue looked like a white halo around his dark hat. They carried on through the heat and humidity for another eighty minutes until they stopped again. This trek was not like their previous ones where they could leisurely amble along and observe the animals, learning about their surroundings and taking photographs of interesting objects. This trek was exhausting because the children were not used to carrying full packs, with enough water and fruit to last them a few days. This was more like a military march, where you have to cover the ground between point A and point B as quickly as possible.

During the water break Terangu gave them more good news, 'This is where it's going to get hard. This next section of the journey takes us through even thicker vegetation. There won't be much of a trail to follow, so stay close and watch out for the tree roots sticking out of the ground. If you trip and injure your ankle it would make this trek impossible. I suggest you get your torches out because the canopy overhead lets very little light through to the forest floor. I'll lead and try to spot any snakes or spiders but hopefully we should only see the non-venomous kind. Follow me children!'

Amy thought that, 'follow me children' or 'look where you are going' would have done just fine. She felt that sometimes Terangu forgot just how young they both were.

George passed his rucksack to Amy and said, 'Don't worry not a number two, just a quick wee before we leave?' as he ducked behind a tree trunk.

'Thanks George, but that's way more information than I needed.' Amy was glad for those extra minutes respite because she was finding it tough going. The ninety percent humidity was smothering her like a heavy blanket. The air in the rainforest was oppressive; it was as if you could reach out and grab hold of it. It felt as though the trees were deliberately trying to slow her progress. Occasionally she suffered from asthma but normally only during the hay fever season. She always carried her inhalers but hoped not to need them today.

Terangu realised his first estimate was wrong. At their current pace it would take closer to six or seven hours to get to the first oxbow lake. Now was not the time to mention his original guesstimate was wide of the mark. He thought it best to keep plodding along until one of them asked, 'Are we there yet?' or 'Is it much further?' He need not have worried about the resilience and fortitude of the young travellers. Amy and George would sweat, struggle, toil and stumble through this sweltering and daunting terrain for as long as it took: even if there was only a wafer-thin chance of rescuing their friend.

Once George got back from his number one, they continued to follow Terangu for an eternity. They tried in vain to enjoy the warble of the birds and the cackle of the cheeky monkeys high above. The sound that drove them on was the crescendo of the frogs. The longer they walked the louder the frogs became and the closer they got to the oxbow lakes. Although they did not mention it, the children's chief concern was that the boat would not be where they predicted. A thought like that could be more energy sapping than the walk itself. It was best to stay positive and try not to think about the worst-case scenario. As many people say about life, it is difficult to stay positive when so many little negative thoughts are running around in your head. Thankfully, Amy and George were together and the exertion from the trek was helping to keep these thoughts locked tightly away.

The croaking frogs kept willing them on hour after hour, drawing them further into the rainforest. When there is no noise from cars, road works or hundreds of people talking at once, nature can be unimaginably loud.

Eventually Terangu slowed up, 'We're almost at the first of the two sites; we must tread carefully and quietly.

The riverbank here has trees along the entire length and they are close to the edge. The fading light, animals' noise and trees will give us plenty of good cover if they have moored here.' They crept forward not batting an eyelid over the vast number of winged friends now active above their heads. Terangu stopped and pointed to the forest floor, 'This is a good sign! Someone has recently buried a bag of salt here and there's a set of footprints leading away in that direction. This is an old poacher's trick to lure animals like tapirs. The tapir licks and eats the soil for the minerals, so the buried salt bag is a big attraction. We must leave here and approach from a different angle, in case they've set up any traps or come back this way to check the bag of salt,' whispered Terangu. He changed direction with the children following his exact tracks to avoid any traps.

They came towards the bank in silence and placing their bags on the floor, crawled on their bellies to a better vantage point. Amy had her binoculars to hand and began to hunt for their quarry. She struggled not to shout for joy as she saw the dirty old boat in the moonlight. It was a wonderful sight, even if it had almost crushed them to death earlier in the day. Amy and George were so relieved to have found the boat. It lifted a weight from their chests because at least the odds of finding Izzy alive were increasing by the minute.

Terangu crawled back to his gear and pulled out the woven mat. They unrolled the mat and lay on their bellies thus deadening the sound of any movement. Using Izzy's binoculars Terangu could make out twenty plus crates and cages at the rear of the boat. He wondered how many animals were in each one and what was hidden below deck?

Very little was going on except smoke was coming out of the main cabin from a small silver chimney. This was cooking smoke and not the thick black plume of engine smoke they had seen this morning. Amy was surprised how quiet all the animals were. What bothered her was that they must have been scared, lonely and hungry; enough reasons for the animals to be quiet and try to avoid any more unwanted attention from the poachers or their local cohorts.

It grew darker and darker around them as night enveloped day. They had not realised how much time had passed watching the boat for clues. Hooknose made a brief appearance on deck, oil lamp in hand and a baseball cap stuck firmly to her head. Amy felt a shiver of tension run down her spine. Hooknose did not look pleased to be carrying out run of the mill jobs, like checking that the mooring ropes were secured to the bank. Once she had gone in, the two locals came out for a cigarette. While they were out on the deck, they double-checked a lot of the sacks and tarpaulins covering the captured prey. Once finished, they went back inside. Terangu signalled for the children to follow him away from their riverbank hiding spot. They picked up their bags and crept a safe distance away to formulate a plan. George, the Boy Scout as ever, pulled a few scraps of paper and a pencil out of the side pocket of his rucksack. Terangu asked Amy to draw a quick sketch of the boat and its position to the nearby riverbank and trees.

'Well children, what do we know so far from spying on them?'

'That must be the toilet because the lights been going on and off since dusk,' George replied, pointing to that room on Amy's sketch.

'I'm sure there must be two sleeping areas inside. The English poachers would want to be separate from the hired help, especially if they are spending weeks onboard together. We know where the kitchen and cabin are located,' said Amy, as she continued to fill in the diagram on the sheet of paper.

'We have to disable the engine or damage the rudder somehow. If something does go wrong, at least they won't be able to motor away with all these poor animals and maybe even us onboard,' suggested George.

'That only leaves drugging the hired help, sneaking onto the boat, trying to locate and free Izzy, freeing the animals and calling for help whilst avoiding being captured and shot. Have I missed anything out?' added Amy.

'I think that covers everything. No worries,' said George, shaking his head.

'George should take the sleeping and laxative draughts up a tree, near the back of the boat. He's the better shot out of the two of us. If the poachers don't come out, maybe George could draw them out with his mimicry of the long-nosed monkeys. Terangu, how long does it take for the drugs to kick in?'

'I'm not sure. I've never made them this strong before. The sleeping draught should sedate someone in thirty minutes or less, if the dart tip is well coated. The laxative should take less time, as it's a strong mix. We'll know when it has taken effect because the toilet light will definitely be on for over ten minutes.'

'I don't know how to disable the boat so I guess that job should go to Terangu, which leaves me to sneak aboard undetected and free Izzy.' George took a sharp intake of breath as Amy's plan began to sink in. 'You both know I can be as quiet as a snake when I have to be. George could give me a torch signal, when it looks safe to go inside. I can find a good hiding place near the front of the boat and wait for the signal. I don't have any ideas about how we call for help, so I'm thinking of trying to free Izzy and then running away. I know it sounds a bit cowardly but if the boat cannot move, then they are stranded until they fix it. This would buy us more time before they could escape, then we could think up a way to free the animals. It isn't the best plan in the world but at least we all do things we're good at,' suggested Amy.

'Are you sure you want to go aboard? I honestly don't mind going,' volunteered George, sounding braver than he actually felt.

'I appreciate the offer but I'm smaller and quieter so I think it's best if I go. If anyone comes near me on deck that I can't see, I'm going to need you to blast them with a couple of darts to give me time to get away,' said Amy, with a hesitant smile.

'I'm going to go and collect vines to use as rope to tie around the rudder. George, I'll leave you with one of my longer blowpipes in case the wind picks up. Here are the two bottles and an extra set of darts as well. All you have to do is open them up and place a dart inside, rotate it around full circle so it gets a good coating on the tip. Please don't make any monkey calls for at least thirty minutes. That will give me and Amy a chance to get into position,' whispered Terangu.

'It will give Hooknose and Hulk more chance to have another drink before they go to bed. With a bit of luck they'll doze off peacefully and we can walk in and out, no problems,' commented George, hopeful as ever.

Terangu pointed at an area on the makeshift map to show them where he would hide once he had disabled the boat. 'I will always be close. If you need me then flash your torches. If it gets bad and you feel in danger then shout and I'll come, I promise! Be brave children and vigilant as a hawk.' He smiled and disappearing into the darkness.

'How can he tell thirty minutes, he hasn't got a watch!' said George softly.

Although this was not the time for humour, Amy certainly appreciated it. If something did go horribly wrong, she would always remember her best friend as being a good laugh. Amy and George had some fruit and water, giving them one last boost of energy before they split up.

George wished her 'Good luck' in a low voice. 'Once you've got Izzy; get out of there. We *will* find a way to free the animals, so try not to worry about them!'

'Thanks George, good luck yourself. Keep your fingers crossed or we could be for the high jump,' murmured Amy, with a half smile.

George gave her a hug and handed her his penknife, 'Having your blowpipe and darts is one thing but they may have stolen the penknife you lent to Izzy. Take mine, just in case.'

Amy smiled at him; put the penknife in her pocket and crawled away afraid to look back as her courage was dwindling. A seed of doubt had been planted in her head. Would she ever see George again? She must concentrate and focus on her job.

George had a lot of stuff and struggled to get up the tree with his torch, binoculars, two blowpipes, two bottles and two different sets of darts. Terangu should not have worried about asking for a thirty minutes head start. It took George this long to get his equipment up the tree. Under normal circumstances he would have scaled this tree with the minimum of fuss; however these were far from normal circumstances. The large tree had lots of useful places to hang and wedge his gear so that it was close at hand. George flicked on the backlight of his watch and thirty-five minutes had elapsed since they split up. It felt strange to wear his watch again; he had not needed it once this holiday. You go to bed when you are tired and get up when it is light or when the animals decide to wake you up.

After waiting a while longer to see if anyone would come out on deck, he decided it was time to put Amy's plan into action. He pinched the end of his nose and started quietly.

'Kee-honk', breath. 'Kee-honk', breath. This continued for over ten minutes until finally, to George's complete surprise, one of the caged long-nosed monkeys responded. He thought that the answer sounded more like a 'kee-clonk, kee-clonk'. He carried on for another few minutes and another nasal call began. 'Kee-hank, kee-hank' was coming from one of the sack-covered cages.

While these two monkeys carried on their calls, George thought he had better get a few darts prepared. He removed the corks from Terangu's elixir and placed two of his smaller darts in each bottle. There was a slight breeze but he did not want to use Terangu's blowpipe unless the wind really picked up. The two monkeys had been joined by a customary 'kee-honk' call from a third monkey, which George thought sounded a lot like his own. He did not have much time to admire the results of his mimicry because the door of the boat opened and the two locals appeared on the rear deck.

'Have you animals learnt nothing since they caught you?' said one.

The other picked up a piece of bamboo and headed for the 'kee-hank' monkey. He lifted the cover and poked the stick inside, 'Remember fur-ball, noise is bad! Peace and quiet is good!' He then rattled his stick along the bars of one of the other noisy monkeys' cages and the clamour soon died down.

'The more noise you make, the more trouble we get in!' said the other.

'I'll be glad when this job is over, so I can get back to some normal work. These two are crazy in the head,' said his frustrated mate, with a sigh.

'Do you want a smoke while we're out? I don't want the boss-lady shouting at me again! Yesterday, she caught me smoking inside and threatened to beat me senseless,' said the smaller man.

The bigger man put down his stick and took a cigarette off him. He lit it, inhaled deeply and coughed unhealthily before telling him a joke, 'A huge orangutan and a baby gibbon were taking a dump from a branch, high up in a tree. The orangutan turns to the gibbon and asks, 'Do you have trouble with poop sticking to your fur?' The baby gibbon smiled at him and replied, 'No trouble at all.' So the orangutan picked the gibbon up and wiped his backside with him.'

They wheezed and chortled amongst themselves, continuing to puff on their foul smelling cigarettes, unaware that George had them in his sights. He was focused, holding his breath, trying to keep his arms from shaking, and then all of his energy went into the short, sharp exhalation.

'Ouch, those blasted mozzies,' said the smaller man, scratching his neck and dislodging the small dart. Bingo, one down and one to go, thought George.

The zither of the cicadas and native frogs croaking had easily drowned out the sound of George firing his first drugged dart. He hastily loaded his second dart into the blowpipe and tried to regain his composure before firing. Luckily, the larger of the two men began talking again.

'I got another one for you, what did the Chinese man say to the Filipino man when he was given his first hot dogOWW!'

'I don't get it!' said the other local, not realising the punch-line was still to come.

'Just forget it. I'm going inside, I hate mosquitoes.' He scratched his neck and went off in a huff.

George felt his muscles relax; he had hit both targets without letting them know he was there. He wanted to flash his torch to where Amy should be hiding, but when he looked through the binoculars he could not see her anywhere. He did not want to draw attention to himself by flashing the torch aimlessly so decided against it. George assumed that Amy must have been close enough to hear the two locals yelp in pain when they were hit by the darts. He guessed that she would then time thirty minutes to wait for the darts to take effect. Otherwise, she would just have to wait until the toilet light was switched on for some time. That would be a giveaway sign. There was nothing more he could do for her now except watch, wait and keep his fingers firmly crossed.

CHAPTER EIGHTEEN

Amy crawled along the riverbank to get into position near the front of the boat. To improve her camouflage, she blackened her face with soft mud. She heard the two local men come out and quieten down the rowdy monkeys. However, she was unsure whether George's darts had found their targets. She waited patiently for the agreed torch signal but it never came. Amy now had to bide her time as she hoped the potent potion was working its way around their bodies.

It had been over thirty minutes since the men had been on deck; Amy was anxious that George had missed his quarry. One worry was soon replaced by another as she saw something moving out of the corner of her eye. She had no intention of being attacked by a reptile and was about to scarper from her muddy hiding place. The memory of Izzy screaming flashed into her mind which strengthened her resolve. She slowly reached for the torch on her belt. She pointed the torch towards the water, being careful to cover the end with her other hand only letting out a sliver of light. She was keen to avoid startling a passing Siamese crocodile or monitor lizard. Her heart rate had risen dramatically and she was holding her breath.

Amy let out a muted sigh of relief, when it became clear what was in the water and immediately switched off her torch. The long, straight spear attached to Terangu's back had misled her into thinking it was a sizeable reptile. He also had rolls of vines on his shoulders and this had helped to transform his appearance. With barely a ripple in the water he had passed by and was soon out of sight around the far side of the boat. Amy was unsure if he had seen her but was pleased to know her friend was close-by.

Finally, a light came on; it was the toilet light. Amy looked at her watch and waited patiently. Five minutes, six minutes, seven minutes passed. The light was still on after ten minutes; Terangu's concoction had had the desired effect. She began steeling herself ready to go on board. Seeing Terangu had boosted her fragile confidence and given her the impetus to begin her part of this foolhardy plan.

Her movements and footsteps were as soft as any predator, be it snake, leopard or raptor. In the blink of an eye Amy had pulled herself on board the boat. The toilet light was still on and she could hear the man inside groaning with pain due to the severity of his stomach cramps. She bit her lip so as not to laugh; he had got what he deserved for being so cruel to the animals. She cautiously edged forward along the side of the boat until she reached the area where the monkeys were being kept. She had to control her urge to take a peek underneath the sacks and tarpaulins to check on the animal's health. 'Concentrate!' she told herself sternly, knowing one mistake and it would be disastrous for them all. Locate Izzy, try to free the animals and if that was not possible then run. Terangu would make sure this hunk of junk boat could not get away but still something was gnawing away at her. She knew in her heart that they could not free Izzy *and* the animals without alerting all on board.

Amy finally reached the main door leading to the inside levels of the boat. This was the moment of truth. Was this to be the shortest rescue mission in history because someone was right behind the door? The door latch screeched slightly as Amy opened the door and peered in. There was very little light so she pulled her scrunched bandanna from her pocket and wrapped it around the end of the torch. When it was securely fastened she pointed the torch to the floor and switched it on. The bandanna had the desired effect; it obscured the torchlight but was still bright enough for her to avoid tripping over anything. Her heart was beating in her throat as well as pounding in her chest. She was trying not to panic but already thought she was making too much noise to get away with this caper. When you try to be quiet, every noise is magnified ten fold.

'Focus you sausage! You've got a job to do,' thought Amy, as she gingerly tip-toed further and further into the boat. Once through the first sitting area, the toilet was next on her right. Amy heard the continued groans and rumblings coming from inside the toilet. Clearly someone still had terrible toilet trouble. This gave her renewed resolve, Terangu had clearly made the laxative too strong but Amy had no sympathy for him. In fact, she would not have thought it out of place to put him in a cage and starve him for a while to see how he liked the treatment dished out to the captive animals.

Amy realised that due to its layout, Izzy was most likely to be somewhere deep in the belly of the boat. She would have to go further below, so took the steps down into the depths of the boat. She came to a corridor where she could instantly see three doors, one on either side and one at the far end. Behind her as she looked down the corridor was a fourth door, a very solid looking door. After pondering her next move she eventually tried the heavy door closest to her. Amy tentatively turned the metal handle waiting for the squeak of the door to awaken the poachers, alerting them to her presence. Putting her shoulder against the door made it open but thankfully the squeak never came. There was a kitchen and storeroom with supplies of noodles, tins, liquor, bottled water and other essentials. She hurriedly snooped around but there was no sign of Izzy. Her fear level was rising and she was finding it more difficult to breathe. It really was a lucky dip, three doors to choose from and Amy knew that two doors were the wrong ones.

Amy warily let herself out of the room, closing it carefully and heading down the corridor. She moved level with the doors on either side of the corridor; the choice became simpler within seconds. You could not have asked for a bigger giveaway than a man snoring like a train. Finally, some luck! At first she was sure it was the Hulk snoring but maybe the sleeping draft had worked so well that it was the drugged local man snoring this loudly. This increased her chances of success; the odds were now a straight 50/50 choice between the last two doors. Amy went towards the door on the opposite side of the corridor. There were no telltale noises inside so she was uncertain whether to try this door or not. Alone and in a very dangerous situation, time stood still.

Not more than a couple of minutes had passed, although it felt as if an hour had passed before she came up with an idea. After checking if there was any noise from the end door, Amy put her nose close to the keyhole. The room had a peculiar smell but at first Amy could not put her finger on it. Was it stinky feet, petrol, old socks or cigarettes? After a moment's reflection, Amy realised it could be a mixture of these smells. This could mean it was the other native helper inside as he was a smoker. Amy had smelt a similar pungent aroma from her hiding spot and realised it was the men having a crafty ciggie. It was also highly likely that he had handled petrol or diesel over the last few days. The other room had a comparable smell meaning Amy was now at a loss to know what to do. She only had one sure-fire method left, lady luck.

Her gut reaction was to go against the smellier of the two rooms and open the one at the far end of the corridor. She had a Malaysian coin deep in her pocket and pulled it out saying to herself; 'If I see a head I go through the smelliest door, if I see wild berries I go to the end door'. When Amy lit her palm she saw berries.

She was relieved that the coin had confirmed her initial feeling.

Before Amy opened the door at the end of the corridor, she tried to hold her breath and listen through the keyhole one last time before entering. She was nauseous with the tension but had come too far to turn back. Was she imagining it or were there now faint noises coming from inside. Was it turning cogs, whirring wheels or maybe even Izzy snoring behind a gag? She could not be sure of anything because her head felt like it was going to explode with the tension. She was sick of this boat already so decided to try the door anyway. Amy gripped the handle firmly with the intention of opening the door as softly as she could. The thought that this was the wrong door and that she might need to make a swift getaway had crossed her mind more than once. Again, she stopped herself going in, something felt wrong. She took her hand off the door handle a millimetre at a time. She went to her belt and removed her blowpipe, putting a single dart inside. If someone other than Izzy was behind this door then at least she could get one silent shot off to buy her a few seconds. Amy was now ready; shoulder against the door and blowpipe in her mouth held between gritted teeth. She turned the door handle with one hand and held her torch with the other. To Amy's complete horror it began to creak. If this was the right door whoever was inside must now be alerted to her presence. She feathered the door open to try to lessen the creaking noise. Not being able to see all the way round the door to have a peek, Amy stepped inside but did not close the door fully behind her.

Once through the door, she used one hand to hold the blowpipe whilst the other shone the dull torchlight around the room. The mechanical noises became more apparent and the smell of oil grew. A new muffled sound emerged from inside the room. The dark bandanna was cutting out too much light, so she loosened it to allow herself a bit extra. It swiftly became clear what or more correctly who was making the indistinct muffled noise. Izzy was facing her but was seated on the floor. She had been gagged and had her wrists bound behind her and was tethered to a metal post.

Amy's heart soared like an eagle. She moved as delicately as she could, all the time trying hard not to let out a shriek of delight. Amy put her blowpipe down in front of Izzy and gave her a big hug. She removed her gag and whispered, 'I'm with George and Terangu. They're outside. Let me untie you.'

Izzy was speechless but well aware of the need for silence. Amy could not untie the ropes that bound Izzy's hands. She took her torch between her teeth and had Georges' penknife out in a flash. The saw blade was useful but the rope binding Izzy's hands was thick and taking much longer than she had imagined. This part of the rescue plan had taken only seconds in her mind but the reality was proving much different.

While Amy was concentrating on trying to cut the rope without cutting Izzy's hands or wrists, she had not noticed the noise of a door opening down the corridor.

Luckily Izzy had heard something, 'Quick, put my gag back in and hide. I think someone's coming!'

Amy immediately did as she was told. Unable to find a hiding place, she crouched down on her knees behind the post to which Izzy was tethered.

She continued frantically sawing away at the ropes until she heard Hooknose muttering, 'Lazy, stinking, good-for-nothing husband of mine. Always leaving me to do the work,' as she pushed her way past the creaking door which Amy had been left slightly ajar. She groped for the light-bulb cord and as she switched it on, she let out a yawn and rubbed the sleep out of her eyes. To Izzy's complete shock she had her rifle in the other hand.

'That drunkard of a husband thought he heard something. Not trying to escape are we?' she asked, knowing full well that Izzy was gagged and could not answer. 'I'm so sick of this stinkin' boat, sick of this country and sick of him snoring his head off every night. I can't wait to get back to civilisation.' Suddenly her eyes came to rest on the floor just in front of Izzy, 'What the hell's that?' she said, pointing to Amy's blowpipe which had been forgotten in the panic.

Amy, who had been obscured by Izzy and the post, had finally managed to cut through the rope. On hearing Hooknose, she whipped her hand round in front of Izzy and grabbed her loaded blowpipe. Before Hooknose could react, Amy fired a dart into her hand. Hooknose dropped the rifle and shock set in as she looked at the dart embedded deeply into her bleeding hand. Her mouth was open but no sound came out. Izzy jumped up and punched her square on the nose with a lethal right hook before she could scream in pain. Hooknose fell to the floor, with an almighty thud and the blood began to flow profusely from her sizeable nose. Izzy would have won that bout by knockout if a referee had been present.

Worried that the thud would wake everyone, Izzy grabbed Amy by the hand, picked up the rifle and sped down the corridor. As they went up the stairs the grey-faced local opened the toilet door to see what the commotion was. Imagine his surprise to find himself staring down the barrel of a loaded rifle.

'Back inside and lock the door!' said Izzy forcefully.

He did not look well before he opened the door but he looked worse having seen the rifle. He meekly closed the door and locked it.

The Hulk opened his door and wandered down the corridor. He pushed the door open and was dumbstruck to find his wife knocked-out on the floor and the hostage gone. He let out an almighty yell and shouted, 'What in hell's name is going on here?'

George was a nervous wreck as Amy had been inside so long. Just then, Amy and Izzy burst out onto the deck. This sudden movement caused George to accidentally release his breath, firing the blowpipe dart he had already prepared. Luckily for Amy and Izzy, his shaky, sweaty hands had made him miss for the very first time. The dart ended up hitting the deck

Amy and Izzy moved as far away from the door as possible.

Izzy barked an order at Amy, 'Jump onto the riverbank. That madman is heading straight for us!' Amy duly obliged, glad to be free from the stinking confines of the poacher's boat.

Izzy backed away from the door and moved so that the animal cages were behind her. She quickly checked to see if the gun was loaded and it was not a second too soon. The door was flung open by the hulking man, almost taking it off its old hinges. His furious anger reached a peak and was now focussed on Izzy.

'Oi, what the devil are ya doin'? Hand that back to me and there won't be no trouble!' he threatened aggressively.

'It's pretty obvious what I'm doing you thick oaf!'

He edged a bit closer towards her.

'Don't take another step, I know how to use this!' countered Izzy, as she took aim at the middle of his humungous chest.

George could not stand the suspense. He took matters into his own hands by firing a succession of small toxic darts into any part of the big man he could hit. He then took out the longer blowpipe and coated one final large dart with the sleeping draught. He let rip with all the puff he had in his lungs and struck gold, hitting the poacher right on his backside.

'Ouch, those damn mosquitoes! They'll be the death of me yet. Okay luv, let's look at this a different way. I don't know why you're so mad at me. It was my wife's idea to take you hostage! I thought we should have left you for the crocs.'

'That's so kind of you. I should probably thank you by giving you back this rifle,' replied Izzy sarcastically. 'You're not helping yourself, you half-wit!'

'Okay, okay! You're not going to shoot me. You're not the type. So let's cut a deal? You know I've got plenty of cash. Whatever currency you want, no problem? Ringitt, Dollars, Euros or Pound sterling. I've got contacts all over the world; they could set you up for life. Be smart for once and fink about it!'

To his surprise a cough came from behind him. He turned his head to see a fierce looking tribesman on the roof of the boat. The old man was pointing some long thin tube directly at his head.

'I suggest you let him bind your hands without any fuss! Otherwise I'll shoot you in the foot with this rifle just because I want to *and* I won't give you the antidote for that!' she said pointing the rifle to something he could not see.

'Antidote for what, what are you going on about?' he shouted.

'It would be an amazing coincidence to get that many mosquito bites in such a short space of time. You've been hit by poisoned darts and will start to feel the effects in a few minutes.'

'Balls! That's a complete crock; I don't believe a word of it! I ain't goin' quietly! I can take you and the old man, even if you're armed.'

'Check your rear end, you great lummox! And don't do anything stupid that you might not live to regret!' said Izzy, deadly serious.

He slowly reached behind him and felt the large dart George had just fired. To his complete horror it was embedded firmly in his butt. The gigantic man appeared to shrink before their eyes. He was not so cocky now he had a poison dart stuck in his rump.

'Okay, okay, tie me up. But do it quick! OW, get this dart out and give me the antidote. I'm startin' to feel woozy!'

Terangu put his blowpipe down and quickly bound the big man using the remainder of the strong vines. Without further delay, he went inside the boat and tied up Hooknose and brought her onto the deck. She was still groggy after being clouted by Izzy. He went in a second time and tied up the local who was still sleeping like a baby, totally unaware of the evening's events. Terangu found some wood and blocked the toilet door so the other local was secured until they could summon help.

Amy and George came back on board the boat before the sleeping draught kicked in. Ricky the Hulk had been hit with enough darts to put a water buffalo to sleep.

George walked over to where he was standing and said courteously, 'I think you've got something that belongs to me?' George used both hands to pluck out the dart that had been firmly wedged in Ricky's rear end. Ricky let out a yell when it came free. 'Sorry old chap! It's not actually poison, so no antidote is needed. Just a little sedative here, a little laxative there and fired by one of your favourite first-class snotty-nosed brats.' George's face was engulfed with a gigantic grin, stretching from ear to ear.

The poacher caught sight of Amy smiling sweetly at him. A look of murder came across his face, 'I swear on my Mum's grave, I'll get revenge on you *both*! Keep lookin' over your shoulders coz this ain't over! I ain't gonna be put away by you two, Hell NO!'

His features were distorted with rage as he screamed obscenities at the children. Each venomous word was delivered with teaspoons of spittle, flying off in all directions, making Ricky look like a rabid dog foaming at the mouth.

Amy suddenly came over all cold. She shuddered at the thought of having made an enemy of this foul-mouthed, wild-eyed madman. This exact moment would be etched in her memory for a long time to come.

Suddenly Ricky's eyes glazed over and his speech became slurred. Amy and George could no longer understand the insults he was hurling at them. His massive head began to loll from side to side and back to front uncontrollably. His eyelids became heavy as the super-size quantity of sleeping draft and laxative coursed its way around his circulatory system.

George was trying hard not to imagine what would happen when Ricky did wake up; the poacher would need an evacuation of the bowels like never before. Now that *would* be messy.

Izzy put the rifle down as soon as the poacher had slumped to the floor, overcome by the powerful concoction. She pulled Amy and George close to her for a hug, 'I'm so proud of you for saving me but ..... cross because you put yourselves in such great danger. Still, it's hard for me stay cross at my rescuers for too long. You'll both be sorely missed from around here when you go home.'

'You didn't think we would leave you behind a second time did you?' joked Amy.

'How would we get to the airport, without *you* giving us a lift?' added George, using his best poker face to cover the laugh that was bursting to get out.

Terangu appeared with some flares that he had found and suggested they set a few off and then try to use the radio inside the cabin to call for help.

'Can we fire the flares, please? I've always wanted to set one of them off but never had the chance. No flare-worthy disasters you see,' asked George.

Terangu looked at Izzy, knowing that after what they had been through, this was a small request. Izzy nodded and smiled obligingly. Amy and George took it in turns to fire these mini-fireworks into the sky, which was becoming brighter by the minute.

'Breakfast anyone? I'll see what they have in the kitchen while you two try to work out the radio,' said Izzy, in an altogether cheerier tone.

Amy and George went inside and inexpertly fiddled with a few dials and buttons trying to send a Mayday message to anyone who might be listening. All they seemed to get was static, so it appeared their luck was beginning to run out. Izzy knocked up some egg sandwiches from the poachers' supplies. The smell drew them from the radio and they went on deck to join Izzy and Terangu for breakfast.

Hooknose was beginning to come round after her KO. She could certainly still feel the pain in her nose and head, 'Oi, don't I get any breakfast, you lazy cow?' she snapped viciously.

'You venomous skaapsteker, I've had enough of your spiteful mouth,' said Izzy, as she put down her plate and went into the cabin. She emerged with the gag they had used on her and then with a struggle she secured it in this rude woman's big mouth.

'I don't think I've heard you curse before?' said Amy.

'It's not a curse but rather a nasty sounding and deadly reptile. It's a famous South African snake with a *huge*, vicious mouth,' said Izzy casually, before finishing off her breakfast. The silence was now truly golden, only broken by the sound of the rainforest coming alive again.

CHAPTER NINETEEN

The sky was turning an exquisite strawberry colour when Terangu saw something that made him choke on his breakfast. Speechless he pointed his hand to a boat coming up the river and eventually spluttered, 'How did they get here so fast?'

Amy picked up her binoculars. 'Excellent, Rigu *is* with them too,' as if she had half expected their arrival.

'Who is 'them' Amy?' asked George excitedly, but he received no answer as Amy was keeping a close eye on proceedings.

It took the vessel a while longer to pull up alongside and Rigu was the first to come aboard. He was bombarded by questions from Terangu, Izzy and George but, before he answered any, he went and gave Amy a big hug.

'Amy, writing your message on that National Parks and Wildlife poaching leaflet was *brilliant*. I thought something strange was going on when I arrived back and no one was around. I found your note and used the mobile phone that I received as a trade for one of my carvings. It took me ages to call these guys because the signal was terrible all around the longhouse. I had to go out in the boat to actually get a call through to them. So, I waited and waited until the Wildlife Enforcement Officers came in the early hours of the morning. I showed them the maps you left behind and we eventually found our way here. The flares were a nice touch though!'

They were overjoyed to see Rigu and the help he had brought. A few of the officers came aboard and were astonished to hear the tale the two children had to tell. If Amy and George had not had two locals to back up their story then the officers would never have believed them. Terangu and Izzy left them to it because they wanted the children to enjoy this moment; they had earned it.

'There'll be a *big* reward for catching this rabble. Let's take some of these covers off slowly so as not to distress the animals any further. I need to check what was captured,' said the head officer.

They counted thirty-nine male and twelve female proboscis monkeys, two baby deer, four large pythons, two young sun bears, a pair of rhinoceros hornbills, a pair of macaques and a male and female pangolin. He carefully opened the hornbills' cage so they could be free at last. The birds did not fly off straight away as expected; they had to practise stretching their wings a few times. Any animal kept in such cramped quarters would need a good stretch.

'Looking at this haul, they were definitely stealing to order. Probably for some millionaire who was trying to build a private collection. Or maybe they were stealing pairs so they could be bred in captivity and then sold for huge profits,' said another enforcement officer.

Amy and George were elated that the monkeys were still alive, albeit very hungry. The children were not so keen to get close to the pythons because they were well-built and agitated at all the goings-on around them. The officer covered up the pythons and then revealed the pangolins to the utter astonishment of the children. Amy and George had no idea how the officer knew which was male and which was female.

'It looks like an armadillo with that protective covering on the outside. I'm relieved they'll go free but so happy that we saw them, almost in the wild,' commented George.

'I've seen their picture in a book but nothing prepared me for how they actually look. Being nocturnal with great camouflage, we'd never have seen one. It's mind-boggling to think we share this planet with so many weird and wonderful creatures,' declared Amy.

They only had a quick peek at the young sun bears because they were distressed and the officer did not want to fully remove the cover. It looked like they had been dragged through the mud when they had been captured. Their coats were matted with dirt and they were in a bad way.

'We'll have to take these bears to the vet before releasing them into the wild. Otherwise, they may not survive having been treated so cruelly,' said the head officer, who was visibly shaking with rage at how all these animals had been manhandled.

Amy loved animals and had been bowled over by seeing all these creatures, but seeing the state of the bears had shaken her up. Amy had something important on her mind; she pulled her best friend to one side so they could speak privately.

'George, we don't really need any reward do we? It's been an incredible experience just trying to help solve the case of the missing long-nosed monkeys. Can I tell them to make sure Terangu gets his share, as that benefits his family? With the other two-thirds of any reward, we should give it to one of the Borneo conservation societies to help protect the proboscis monkeys or even split it with the orangutan rehabilitation centre?'

George looked disappointed but tried desperately hard not to; even though in truth he would have loved a new mountain bike or a top-of-the-range laptop.

Amy continued, 'We've had a bucket load of fun, learnt masses about the environment and we're alive. Besides, Hooknose and the Hulk *are* English poachers.'

George smiled, 'Hmmm! Not really cricket to take a reward when this trash came from *our* country. This has been one memorable adventure and we've had a good giggle. Anyway, it's hardly cost a penny!' George let out a big sigh, 'I suppose I won't miss what I never had.'

Amy gave him a hug and a peck on the cheek. She then went off to explain the situation to the head enforcement officer.

Terangu turned up soaking wet and told them he had removed his spear and the vines from around the rudder, so the boat could now be towed away.

Izzy returned to the boat with Terangu's woven basket on her back filled with young shoots, flowers and leaves to feed the animals. The head officer came over and asked if the children wanted to ride with them or with the animals until they reached suitable release sites along the Kinabatangan River. Izzy answered on their behalf, as she knew they would want to feed the hungry proboscis monkeys.

Rigu helped the officers check all the ropes tied to the large vessel in order to tow it down the river. The other officers began to move the four prisoners on to their powerful patrol boat.

Ricky the hulking poacher looked punch-drunk, but came round enough to shout, 'Oi posh brats. Know what the fine is for hunting without a license? 18,000 ringitt! I can pay that now. You'd better look out! I'll get off and come hunting for *you* next time!'

The look of horror on both of their faces gave him a great deal of pleasure. Ricky started a belly laugh that would have shaken a smaller boat. His obese frame was wobbling like jelly.

Izzy acted immediately, 'Quiz question for you, funny man. Did you read the next line of the rulebook? Hunting on its own attracts a fine plus a 'possible jail sentence'. However, if you intended trafficking these animals to another country then that's a *different* matter. I think the officers might be interested in some of the paperwork and phone numbers I found. Oops, sorry! Did I forget to mention that I snooped through *all* your stuff earlier? If they prosecute you for trafficking, then you're looking at 16 years in jail. You can throw in kidnap and attempted murder for your crazy ramming antics! Oh and finally, I think the bullets in your rifle will match the one that I removed from an orangutan the other day. The fine will be the least of your worries. You should be worried about what the inside of a foreign jail cell looks like! You're not laughing anymore?'

Amy and George were beaming from ear to ear. 'By the way you goon, we're not posh or rich! We won this holiday on a packet of Choco-Snaps. We were just lucky to have bumped into you,' said Amy mockingly. She was so glad that this would be her last encounter with this loathsome, hulking individual.

As ever, George could not resist one last dig, 'Please be careful in that jail. I hear it's a jungle in there, especially if you're on your own!' He then winked at him.

Ricky's grogginess disappeared; he began violently kicking, screaming and trying desperately to get to George but to no avail. He was brusquely bundled aboard the patrol boat by all the officers. Amy and George smiled and waved to him, as if he were going away for a weekend's vacation. Rigu then cut the rope which was holding them to the riverbank.

One of the younger officers called Henry came across, 'There's nothing like the sight of an old enemy who is down on his luck.'

'Is that a quote from someone famous?' enquired Amy, intrigued.

'No idea, I heard it on the TV,' answered Henry, as he walked off to look for more evidence around the boat.

The children looked at each with a grin before continuing to tend to the needs of the animals. The pangolins were soon released back into the rainforest and moved much quicker than either of them expected. It took most of the day to tow the boat back upriver but it was well worth it. Amy and George were allowed to assist the wildlife officers in the release of the rare primates, the proboscis monkeys. When Amy saw them form into groups high up in the branches it brought her to tears. George put his arm around her shoulder as they enjoyed the highlight of the trip together. All the males let out mighty 'kee-honks', as if it was a call to let the others in hiding know they were safely home. Soon other monkeys could be heard, far off in the distance answering their brothers.

Even in the short time they were watching, a mother with a baby clinging to her underside came out of the rainforest to join them. They felt this was the moment when the primate puzzle was finally solved.

Amy and George wanted to stay longer to savour this moment but the officers had to take the criminals away. As they were drawing up towards the entrance of the small tributary, Izzy noticed her boat tied up by the bank.

'Sorry I didn't ask if I could borrow it,' said Rigu. Izzy just smiled and nodded understandingly at him.

The wildlife enforcement officers thanked Amy and George profusely for their bravery and resourcefulness. Izzy, Terangu, Rigu, Amy and George were all helped into Izzy's boat. The officers waved and wished Amy and George a safe flight home. This minor fact had been well and truly forgotten in the hullabaloo of the last few days.

'Time truly does fly when you're having fun,' said Amy, with a big smile.

Izzy stopped off at the longhouse to drop off Terangu and Rigu. Before they were about to push off, Amy thanked them again, 'Thanks for everything, we could never have done this without you! We'll both miss you, your family and the longhouse very much.'

The three friends motored off back towards their home base. Tiredness was more than just creeping over them. It was bounding over them rapidly, especially after a sleepless night, hellish trek and a full-on adventure behind them. When they arrived back at the lodge, Izzy thanked them all over again for coming to her aid. She apologised to Amy over the loss of her penknife. Hooknose had taken it from her when she was first captured. Later Izzy had searched the boat to find it but to no avail. Amy politely turned down her kind offer of a replacement knife.

Neither of the children had any appetite for dinner; George must have been dead tired to turn food down. Izzy tucked them into bed in a motherly fashion. Amy and George were sound asleep in a matter of minutes. Izzy was also exhausted after her ordeal but just managed to set her alarm before collapsing into her bed.

CHAPTER TWENTY

Had they been asleep long? Could it have been a vivid dream? These questions came into Amy's mind, as she woke up to the familiar smell of eggs cooking. When she saw the floor of their room strewn with torches, blowpipes, darts, a penknife and dirty dark clothes, she knew it must have been real. She felt her cheeks and they were still slightly caked with mud. She opened the shutters and let the morning light in, which promptly woke George up.

'Are you okay, sleepy head?'

'A little stiff from the trek and sitting up that tree for so long, but I'm fine. Oh, except for one thing. I'm absolutely ravenous!' replied George.

'Well that's nothing new! You're always hungry George. Let's go and see what Izzy is cooking and get cleaned up later?'

'Good idea! I don't mind if either of us smells bad but I do mind if my stomach is rumbling. Let's go Sherlock,' replied George, cheerier at the prospect of food. They soon found Izzy preparing a smashing final breakfast for them.

'That's good timing. I was about to call you. I borrowed a few bits and pieces from their boat yesterday. I don't suppose the poachers will need all this where they're heading. At least not for the next few decades anyway!' joked Izzy, to the delight of the children.

They chatted over breakfast until Amy finally said, 'The punch that floored Hooknose was a real peach. You should go pro Izzy!'

'I wish I'd been there to see you deck her,' added George.

Izzy was silent for a moment before replying, 'I wouldn't normally condone violence and I would hate to see either of you copy my actions *but* on this occasion that wicked woman got what she deserved!'

'We promise not to get in any fights Izzy, unless of course it's with gun carrying poachers,' replied George, with a cheeky grin.

Izzy did not want the meal to end because then they would have to wash, pack and go to the airport. However, this roller coaster of a holiday had to come to an end. The children still had the energy to ask Izzy questions all the way to the airport. They had to fill in the blanks in their flora and fauna journals that they had kept during the holiday. This helped because it kept Izzy occupied and also stopped the children feeling sad at having to leave Malaysia behind. They would never forget the extraordinary magic of Borneo!

Let us gloss over the parting exchanges because it is guaranteed that many tears were shed. Anyone who has ever said goodbye to a close friend or family member at the airport will know how upsetting it is.

The children promised to stay in touch and thanked Izzy for her kindness. They were again escorted to their first class seats but this time it was with mixed feelings. They were looking forward to seeing their families but it was unbelievable that their 'once in a lifetime' experience was now over. They drank their complimentary orange juice and ate well but dozed for most of the flight. The flight attendants tucked them in with extra blankets and pillows, so they were well looked after.

When they finally touched down in England they both felt surprisingly refreshed. Aeroplanes can be uncomfortable on long haul flights, especially if you are tall and in economy class or 'cattle class,' as some rude passengers around them called it. Fortunately, Amy and George were short and in First-Class so this did not apply. They collected their baggage and a kindly flight attendant ensured they were quickly waved through customs. This was very fortunate indeed considering they both had blowpipes, darts and other paraphernalia inside their luggage. Both sets of parents were at the airport Arrivals gate, straining for a glimpse of them. Andy Cooke had hired a minibus so both families could travel to and from the airport together. The children were immediately smothered with hugs and kisses when they were finally reunited with their families.

Both Kelly and Helen were horrified at *most* of the tales they were told but thankful Amy and George had come back in one piece. Tom and Andy were happy that they had made good use of their penknives, even if one had been lost.

The children tried to spend the next few days relaxing but their younger siblings Bethany and Vincent constantly pestered them with questions. They also began seeing close friends and completing their personal diaries. A big family party was soon to be held to celebrate their return.

On the morning of the party, a special delivery arrived at the Applegate household addressed to the competition winner – Miss Amy Applegate. Inside the package there were some foreign newspapers cuttings, two expensive-looking velvet cases and four envelopes. Two of the envelopes were marked for the attention of Master George Cooke. Amy decided to wait until George, Andy, Helen and her two sisters Liz and Sophie arrived for the party before opening anything.

Once the whole family had congregated and the children had been overwhelmed with hugs and kisses, George and Amy discussed what they should open first. Amy only had eyes for the regal-looking purple velvet cases. They snapped open the boxes at the same time to find a gleaming solid gold engraved medal in each, with a handwritten note. The note read as follows: -

Dear Amy / Dear George,

The Malaysian Government, covering the States of Sabah and Sarawak in Borneo, would like you to accept our highest award for bravery. Your exceptional acts of courage in the face of danger and your boundless generosity to local charities must be recognised.

You will always be welcome in our country and we offer you our sincere thanks and deepest appreciation for your deeds. We look forward to your next visit and hope you will find the time to visit us in Kuala Lumpur.

Signed,

The Prime Minister

Well, that was not a bad start on the present front! Kelly and Helen duly placed the medals around the children's necks as the family cheered. They then each opened an envelope from the Managing Director of the Asian branch of Choco-Snaps Cereals. He spoke of his delight at the bravery medals and told them that their story had appeared in the Bangkok Post, the Kuala Lumpur Times and even the Singapore Today newspaper. One of the wildlife enforcement officers had 'accidentally' leaked their acts of bravery to these English-speaking newspapers. Their heroic and selfless acts then proceeded to appear in every other paper in South East Asia and would certainly be picked up by the English press. Therefore the cereal company wanted to offer them each $50,000 due to the positive publicity the company had received. You could have blown them over with a feather. Amy and George had not expected this. They did not know how much one US Dollar was worth in pounds but it sounded a lot. Tom went to the kitchen drawer and got the calculator to work out the exchange rate for them. He told them they each had over £30,000 pounds to spend, more than enough for a new bike at least!

Warning bells were instantly going off inside Amy's head! Hooknose and the Hulk would not have to look hard to find them, if they did ever get out of jail. All this press would not help to keep her and George safe. However, this was a time for enjoyment not anxiety so she tried to put it to the back of her mind.

The last envelopes contained a similar thank you letter from the Chief Executive of Flyaway Airlines. In the letter they were called 'young ambassadors of their country', which they loved the sound of. The Airline offered to fly them both *anywhere* in the world once a year until they were eighteen. This offer came with a message saying that they would like to interview the pair and take photographs for the staff magazine once in a while. This did not seem like too much of a hardship to get to travel anywhere on the planet once a year. The family looked at the newspaper cuttings and re-read the letters. No mother or father or sister or brother or aunt or uncle could have failed to be delighted at their triumph. When asked by their family where they might like to go next, Amy and George kept their thoughts to themselves.

It might spoil their Mums' day to learn how far and wide they hoped to travel next summer holiday, especially after so many near misses this trip. Amy wanted to visit Tasmania to catch a glimpse of a Tasmanian devil or see the wonders of the Galapagos Islands in South America. George had very big reptiles on his mind, he was thinking about the dinosaur-like Komodo Dragons in Indonesia. The world was now officially their oyster.

How did two children turn out to be so fortunate? That is the funny thing, because even ordinary children can find bravery through each other's friendship. If you mix a willingness to learn, ability to adapt to new surroundings along with some kind and inspirational people, you have a potent concoction.

ACKNOWLEDGEMENTS

A number of people have contributed to this book but one more than any other. This book has been made infinitely better by having the illustrations of Bethanie Cunnick throughout (plus designing the front cover). Bethanie has also given her time and work for free so that we can raise as much money as possible for my chosen charity (Great Ormond Street Hospital for Sick Children).

I would like to thank my parents, Helena and David, whose support made world travel possible. Their kindness and guidance has enabled me to fulfil my ambition to research and write a children's book. I must also express my gratitude to all of the guides, workers, helpers and volunteers at the following establishments in Borneo, Malaysia:

Gomantong Caves Information Centre
Sepilok Orangutan Rehabilitation Centre
Sarawak Cultural Village near Kuching
Sarawak Museum, Kuching

Sabah Museum - Kota Kinabalu
Bako National Park
Niah Caves National Park
Crocker Range National Park
Similajau National Park
Kinabalu National Park
Tabin Wildlife Reserve
Lambir Hills National Park
Danum Valley Conservation Centre
Tambunan Rafflesia Reserve
All of my friends from the Sukai River Lodge.

Numerous guides and workers at the National Parks have helped me to gain an insight into the wide variety of animal, insect and plant life that appear in this book. I must express my appreciation to the kind, generous and knowledgeable peoples of both the Malaysian states of Sabah and Sarawak. They have enriched my journey across thousands of kilometres of their magnificent country. I hope many other people get to enjoy the majestic wildlife and fascinating culture of Borneo.

My mother and my aunt, Norma Williams, deserve a special mention for reading through many draft manuscripts, editing and checking the grammar. My partner, Anna, and her sister, Elizabeth, have also helped greatly in this department. Anna deserves a medal for putting up with me whilst I've juggled two jobs and been working on this in the evenings, weekends and on holiday. I would like to salute Simon Moore for all of his help and encouragement whilst I was trying to get the book published. I owe you and Mike Hampton (web designer and an old friend) a few cold ones!

Two great friends have given up so much time to help me with the audio book version. Jack Hook (producer and sound engineer) and his brother Max (who read it and provided all the character voices), have ensured that many children across the world will get to hear this story. It sounds excellent, you two are legends! If **ANY charities who deal with sick children or adults with learning disabilities** want the Ebook or audio book computer files to distribute for FREE, please email me at:

oliver.nash@theprimatepuzzle.com For more information about the audio book, author, illustrator or where to purchase the book please go to my website; www.theprimatepuzzle.com

If you have been given a copy of this book as a gift or found it in a charity shop, library, school and want to donate to Great Ormond Street Hospital for Sick Children Charity, please check out www.justgiving. com/theprimatepuzzle

As Albert Einstein once said, "Only a life lived for others is a life worthwhile."

Lightning Source UK Ltd.
Milton Keynes UK
UKHW012140050921
389958UK00001B/59